MAR - - 2016

W9-CUU-166

THE PLIMSOLL LINE

MAR - - 2010

THE PLIMSOLL LINE

JUAN GRACIA ARMENDÁRIZ

Translated from the Spanish by
Jonathan Dunne

Hispabooks Publishing, S. L.
Madrid, Spain
www.hispabooks.com

All rights reserved. No part of this book may be reproduced in any form
or by any means without permission in writing by the publisher except
in the case of brief quotations embodied in critical articles or reviews.

Copyright © 2008 by Juan Gracia Armendáriz

Originally published in Spain as *La línea Plimsoll* by Editorial Castalia, 2008
First published in English by Hispabooks, 2015
English translation copyright © by Jonathan Dunne
Copy-editing by Cecilia Ross
Design © simonpates - www.patesy.com
Cover image, Water Vortex © Stocksnapper / Dreamstime.com

ISBN 978-84-942830-9-3 (trade paperback)
ISBN 978-84-943496-0-7
Legal Deposit: M-35873-2014

For my father, Carlos, in memoriam.

Happiness, like everything human, is unstable.

ADOLFO BIOY CASARES

AUTHOR'S NOTE

The "Plimsoll line" is a mark indicating the maximum limit to which a ship may be loaded. During the second half of the nineteenth century, shipping companies would fill their ships with loads that exceeded their capacity. In the case of shipwreck, the companies would collect the ship's insurance settlement. This phenomenon was known in Great Britain by the name of *coffin ships*. Samuel Plimsoll (Bristol, 1824–Folkestone, 1898) gained fame for spearheading a peculiar legal battle aimed at denouncing this practice and improving conditions for seamen. In 1873 the British parliament decreed that all ships had to indicate their waterline with what has become known as the Plimsoll line or Plimsoll mark.

During the Second World War, psychologists from the US army borrowed this concept for personality tests, to measure the limit beyond which an individual could no longer be subjected to disturbing emotions. Such tests were designed to select those individuals whose Plimsoll line made them more suitable for occupying positions that demanded great emotional resilience.

1

Were it not for the oak forest flanking and hiding it, the house would not draw the attention of an anonymous observer, being as it is a tiny relief in the topography of the valley, little more than a banal and therefore human gesture in the landscape extending north. It could be said the house survives as a parasite, camouflaged beside a forest that now, in the midst of winter, is just a tangle of cold, black branches. That may be why the forest would only attract the attention of an observer with a certain ecological bent and would otherwise pass unnoticed. Like the house, in fact. A free-standing home with three floors and a functional, Nordic design that would have stood out several years ago, when the most expensive dwellings continued to be the old villas belonging to the capital's middle classes—houses draped in sumptuous ivy; damp rooms; lowered blinds—and the city had yet to spread outward in sprawling residential zones. An anonymous observer could infer that the land where the house is built was once—perhaps forty or fifty years ago—an area covered in massed trees. At that time, there was nothing in the valley to suggest the fields of grain that light it up with greens, yellows, and ochers, depending on the season, or the plowing, grazing, and subsequent repopulation of pines that today are being meticulously devoured by processionary caterpillars.

The house forms a detail that is in harmony with this remaining trace of primitive woodland, stuck close to it, almost concealed, despite the iron weathervane, the chimney, and the slate roof. This mimicry seems to afford the house less protection than isolation. The anonymous observer might deduce that the house will be further concealed in a few months' time, when the forest begins to feed on the warmth of the sun, because it will then disappear behind the shadows of foliage and the golden reflections of leaves, and only by taking an aerial photograph of the valley will it be possible to confirm that there really is a house down there, among the trees.

Safely positioned at the edge of the forest, having slowly crossed the slightly putrid stench of earth, perhaps causing a thrush dozing in the fork of a branch to fly away, the anonymous observer would judge the house's garden to be small, even too small compared to the sylvatic proximity of the forest, and that this meanness delimited by fencing is accentuated by a lawn cut with the surprising pulchritude of a golf course, a bright green horizontality interrupted by only two objects: a hoe abandoned next to some hydrangeas, and a sack of fertilizer with part of its contents heaped in a corner. On the porch, the wicker chaise longue with its apple-green neck cushion and the binoculars suggest the presence of an inhabitant in dialogue with the surroundings. But near the table, the gardening gloves placed hand over hand in an empty plant pot, the rough-hewn cane, the ashtray overflowing with used butts, and the crossword magazine all point to leisure, even convalescence, as if the owner of these objects had nothing better to occupy his time with in winter than doing puzzles, going for walks around the area, trying out a new method for grafting hydrangeas, or keeping a watch on the movements of birds and atmospheric changes. The dirtiness of the ground—the dried leaves piled up in a corner, the bird droppings, and the muddy footprints entering and leaving the house— seems to indicate gardening activities carried out with both urgency and a lack of interest, a far cry from the serenity of spirit that would seem to be required for the maintenance of a small, bourgeois, solitary garden.

Having abandoned the shelter of the last branches and become reconciled to the north wind beating the leaves, the observer might judge that there is indeed nothing extraordinary about the porch, including the Mexican ceramic plates under which, on a canvas chair, a fat tabby cat is taking a nap, adding a domestic touch of quietude to the entrance. Despite the cold, the animal keeps watch, between its eyelids, over the lawn's perfect horizontality, suppressing its atavistic desire to hunt beneath a falsely stoic attitude and waiting for the mole's snout to appear over by the hydrangeas, maybe, or perhaps on the other side, next to the heap of fertilizer. Two nights previously, it felt the mole digging with the muffled beat of displaced earth, drawn by the watery odor of earthworms, which have proliferated recently in the garden. It narrows its gaze in order to calm its predatory anxiety and shades its eyes, which are a poisonous green color, from the evening light. It will catch the sapping mole, maybe not today or tomorrow, but it will eventually gnaw its leathery flesh, put it to death as it has so many other rodents that, having arrived from the other side of the fence, have been trying for some time to annex the garden to their natural hunting grounds. It will not kill it out of a spirit of service or hygiene but in order to indulge a need that is in no way satisfied by the infrequent, puerile games its owner proposes on rare afternoons by throwing a ball of aluminum foil down the hallway. Nor does the stray dog that hangs around in the vain hope the man will toss it some leftovers sate the neutered cat's now slender impulses. The mutt contents itself with barking raucously from the other side of the fence, revealing chipped canines and a ribcage stuck to its skin, and the cat simply gazes out from the chaise longue in the knowledge the dog will soon grow tired, its lower lip dripping with large gobbets of saliva, its barks grown hoarse and weak. Then, less out of a desire to make a futile gesture of territoriality than to fulfill an ancient ritual of natural enmity, the cat abandons its post, arches its back, bristles, and takes a few steps to one side, thereby reigniting the dog's agonizing barks, in order to slope off in search of somewhere quieter. Now, however, lying on the deckchair, it merely licks its fur in the certainty the mole will satisfy its waning predatory instincts, having discovered, with a prick to its feline sense of pride, that the blackbirds—those birds that were once the object of its juvenile, venatorial leaps and whose population it has decimated over the years—have taken to mocking its sluggish approaches and flying off without alarm, safely out of reach. After various unsuccessful attempts, it stopped attending to its hurt pride and directed its hunting abilities toward less skillful opponents. Since then, moles, moths, and the odd grasshopper have been more than enough to fulfill its athletic aspirations. It senses the anonymous observer approaching in the evening light, moving diagonally toward the column on the porch, but that shadow attracts its attention about as much as a man out for a Sunday walk, or a mushroom forager. It notices the observer without a flicker of surprise, with the classist, feline haughtiness it shows Jeremías whenever he bursts into the house, filling it with the stench of brandy, gasoline, and the elements, depositing his toolbox on the kitchen table, and saying *kitty, kitty* to it while rubbing his fingers together as if in search of a tip. It could be said the observer is a guest of the light, a visage of air.

Viewed from the porch by pressing one's nose against the glass and shading one's eyes with one's hand, it can be seen that the inside of the house is not crude but combines good taste and ostentation. The living room looks to the observer like the late reflection of a personality divided against itself, obliged to unite inclinations that can only be reconciled with difficulty—social acceptance, whose calling cards are the English liquor cabinet, a terracotta, a silver tray, and a zebra skin spread out on the floor; and cultured, not to say progressive, heterodoxy, an impulse championed by a vaguely phallic aluminum sculpture and a white, spherical bust like an ostrich egg, the image of which is doubled by the entryway mirror. The house could well be a candidate nominated to feature in some glossy publication specializing in interior design. "Risky And Conventional," "Avant-Garde Without The Razzmatazz," or "Tradition And Gestural Daring" might be the title of such a report.

Inside, the arrangement of objects is overseen by the portrait of a woman with an asymmetrical face, prominent forehead, and rounded shoulders whose gaze, although austere, does not express matriarchal severity so much as it does orphanhood, a feature that seems to extend to the tension in the arms and the hands resting on the lap of her blue dress. In contrast with other, smaller paintings flanking it on the wall—St Mark's Square in Venice glimpsed through the mist; a seascape with small boats on an ocean of impossible transparencies—the anonymous observer would judge the portrait to be inaccurate but faithful, in keeping with the atmosphere of a house that offers itself as readily to the light as to the dark. In fact, outside, the sunlight declines rapidly, casting the room into sudden shadow, as if somebody had turned down the spotlights at an exhibition, because in the distance, several storm clouds like soiled cotton balls have detached themselves from the ridge of mountains, a solid, violet line rising oblivious to the protection it affords the valley, to which it nevertheless grants the privilege of a microclimate combining Atlantic bucolicism and Mediterranean luminosity. This may have been one of the reasons that drove the owner to build a home out of town at a time when nobody in the city dared commit such mortgaging madness, and that may have been what determined where the house was to be erected, in a no-man's-land between an alfalfa field and an oak forest. The ravine already existed—a spit of bags, pieces of rubble, and rusty machine parts, overrun by nettles—but, quite logically, the owner must have thought the ugliness of the ravine would be offset by the proximity of the oaks. Besides, it was possible to access the highway via a local road that started at the gas station and ended four miles further on, next to a tiny, abandoned railway station that freight trains passed through without stopping. Furthermore, the forest was so close it was possible to touch the branches of the trees from the windows. In reality, the house is a solitary spot, like a small island, and shouldn't draw the attention of an anonymous observer at all.

The *ring-ring* brings the telephone back to life with the vibrations of a mechanical insect, a black beetle that spreads its wings and flies over the side table, dodges the blue sofa, crosses the dining table, bounces against the old earthenware, passes in front of the mute gesture of the woman in the portrait, at the height of her chin—it could be said the woman's eyes follow the beetle's precocious flight—and then heads diagonally across the living room in order to finally ascend the stairwell leading to the third floor of the house. Up there, another telephone replies in a shriller tone. The beetle returns to the living room, flying along the ground with no time to stop, because the telephone starts ringing again and the other phone upstairs replies to its call after a short delay. The process is repeated another two times without anybody picking up the phone, at which the beetle, feeling exhausted and being followed attentively by the gaze of the woman in the portrait, returns to its quietude as an object on the table. A weary voice reads out a message on the answering machine tape. *"Hello, I can't come to the phone right now. If you'd like to leave a message, please do so after the tone. Thanks."* An automatic beep announces the start of the recording. On the other end of the line, there is the background noise of street sounds, prominent among them the wailing of a siren. Somebody clears their throat, allows a few seconds to pass until the sound of the siren disappears in the traffic of the city. *"Hi, it's Ana. I'm sorry I couldn't go and see you at the clinic, but we have to meet. I spoke to my lawyer yesterday. He says now is a good time to find a buyer, interest rates are going to come down, and apparently that will boost the property market. He says it won't be difficult to find somebody interested in the house and we can ask for a good price. You know I don't understand much about these things, so it would be good if we could talk as soon as possible . . ."* There is a syncopated hum. The car horns add an impression of urgency to the woman's words. *"I think my battery is running out. Why don't you buy yourself a cell phone, like everybody else, or get an email account? I hope you're OK. Call me. Talk to you soon."* The tape stops, and a second beep indicates the end of the message. The silence of the room takes on a more obvious presence, and everything would settle back into tepid penumbra were it not for the fact that on a corner of the side table, next to the beetle and the answering machine, a red light is blinking.

The anonymous observer could deduce that the tone of the message does not coincide with the features of the woman in the portrait, as if in the time that has elapsed between the painting of the portrait and the phone call, the woman had undergone an intimate metamorphosis, the effects of which have already surfaced in her voice and features, in such a way that the portrait would need to be retouched in order to remain faithful to its model. This change is no doubt reflected in the sonorous tone of her voice, which is surely not what it was when she posed in a blue dress, with bare shoulders, three hours a week for a month in the studio of a local painter. That face would seem to require a less youthful voice, one without a trace of humor. On the table in the entryway, various photographs have been arranged in a fan shape, a feminine touch that does not, however, appear to extend to the atmosphere of the house, as if the woman in the portrait were a gaunt presence whose shadow is projected only on small, mute objects that, from corners, drawers, and cupboards, in nooks and crannies, seem to want to vindicate her through a bond of silence. The ringing of the phone has died down in the living room, absorbed by the density of the shadows. It could be said that the space of the living room has returned to its previous, precarious equilibrium.

There may be nobody at home; if there is somebody, it's impossible to tell, and the anonymous observer could stop now at the photographs in the entryway with the same attitude that might be adopted by an inopportune visitor—rocking on his feet, his hands clasped behind him, feeling a little embarrassed because his arrival has interrupted a family meal, an intrusion he attempts to mitigate by gazing at the faces in the photographs, apparently oblivious to the fragments of conversation and domestic noise proceeding from the dining table— who, once his visit is over, takes his leave, asking them to forgive the interruption and enjoy their meal, his hand raised in the doorway. But now there are no familial clinks of plates and forks, no traces of words or laughter, and unlike any other visitor, the observer remains in the entryway, gazing at the family photographs, there being nothing to indicate he has any intention of leaving.

In one photograph, a man, a woman, and a girl form an equilateral triangle. The shape stands out against a background of unfocused lawn, since the zoom, its attention on the faces, has turned the grass into an impressionistic blur, and a light bathes all three in a golden glow, possibly autumnal—a simple, skillful optical effect that less expert hands would have spoiled, condemning the photograph to the aesthetics of a shampoo advertisement. All three smile at the lens. The man occupies the triangle's upper vertex and stretches out his arms toward the two women in a paternal gesture, resting his hands on their shoulders, one on his wife, the other on his daughter. Closely cropped, grayish hair, bags under his eyes, and still-flexible skin are the features of a man aged around fifty, attractive, dressed casually for a Sunday outing, satisfied, perhaps, with what he has achieved, at least that's what can be deduced from his smile, his squinting eyes turned toward the camera, which he possibly can't see, blinded by the evening's golden light, and the relaxed gesture with which his arms embrace the two women, leaning forward so he is at their height. On the right, the woman with dark blond hair is a less clement replica of the woman in the portrait. Neither the zoom nor the shutter have been kind to her, her face is long and thin, skin hanging off her cheeks, and the light, which on the other faces acquires an optimistic quality, on hers appears frozen, as if the photographer had managed to reveal a tiredness that had been accumulating in her features for quite some time. On the left, the girl wears an expression of incredulity. A surly gesture which, far from belying her age, emphasizes it with exultant obviousness—sixteen, perhaps seventeen, a still slightly masculine slenderness, and like her father, she also flashes the half-smile of a well-brought-up teenager who smiles because that's what Uncle Óscar has asked her to do, camera at the ready, urging her to join her parents because "it'll make a good photo, just look at the light, that's it, like that you're all perfect," which forces her to drag her chair over to her mother's and straighten herself up against the metal back. While her father follows the advice of her uncle and stands behind them, the girl puffs at her bangs, moistens her lips with her tongue, a little dazzled by the sun, worried by two thoughts that rapidly cross her mind: that her sweater is going to reveal the now definitive size of her breasts, and that she should tilt her head a little in order to disguise the blackhead that appeared under her lip the night before. "Come on, Laura, smile," somebody says, and she smiles, and the three of them say *cheese* in unison, at the exact moment she feels her father's hand pressing down on her shoulder and hears the click of her irritating Uncle Óscar's camera. The observer, however, steps back, moves away from the photograph, and the three characters in the portrait return to their initial hieratic state, frozen in the evening light, their mouths open and jovial, there being heard now the groan of a mattress spring followed by a dry cough, a long yawn, and another cough, sounds that indicate someone upstairs has just awoken.

The man opens his eyes. Bewildered, it takes him awhile to focus on the tiny crack that looks like a crater, over there, in the distance—a wrinkled spot lost on the pearl-colored wall stretching out in front of him, imitating a lunar landscape. The surface appears immense, as if when he opened his eyes, everything had taken on a novel quality it previously lacked, and so the space stretching between the tip of his nose and the pearl-colored wall is now a vacuum vibrating up and down, full of light, extending toward him and folding him in. The man feels he might explode and that *that* is getting mixed up with him, with his swollen eyelids, his hair stuck to his brow, the old sweat impregnating the sheets. For a moment, everything seems to emerge from the tiny crack in the wall, a muffled bellow that could demolish the partitions in the house and his consciousness. He feels he could cross through the air or disappear effortlessly until he attained the quietude of that tiny crater. Without fear. The man shudders, coughs again, and the impression of plenitude vanishes as soon as he realizes it's still day outside and that under the pillow, he still feels pain in his arm from the injections. He senses he is still accompanied by a fragment of his last dream, of which all he can remember is a stranger's smile and the pleasant impression of having flown over the valley. The crack in the wall regains its mute, insignificant appearance, as does the glass of water, the thirty pills of different sizes and colors, selected, one by one, from among barbiturates, sedatives, and sleeping pills, the alarm clock under the extinguished lamp on the bedside table . . . Suddenly, these objects seem to adapt to a closer world, within hand's reach.

He could repeat the same words, even parodying the severe, pedagogical tone his wife had used to tell him she was leaving him—"I've thought about it, I've considered it at great length, and now I know it without a shadow of a doubt. I want to end this. I want to go. We're finished . . . we were finished a long time ago. You do realize, don't you? It's the best thing for both of us. And Laura would agree. Laura wouldn't be happy seeing us like this." While he doesn't remember his answer, he does remember the first impression caused by these words uttered without drama in a restrained tone that could only be the result of practice and, therefore, of a well-planned strategy—a soft but heavy blow in the pit of his stomach that sometimes, when he awakes, like now, he recalls for no reason. That's when the succubus of his bad dreams seems to prolong its habitual presence and remain seated on his chest, fully awake still, and watch him, leaning forward with the old smile of a Gothic creature, the expression of an elderly child that may just as easily dissolve into hysterical laughter as pull faces like a circus monkey or adopt poses indicating sadness, self-pity, or obscene grimaces of pleasure. The man twists his body, stretches out his pained arm, and the mattress springs creak again beneath the weight of his hip. With the heavy flight of an ugly bird, the succubus flaps over to the bedhead. It may stay there for the rest of the day, or only until the man leaves the room. It sometimes alights on his shoulder and accompanies him in his daily tasks, like a parrot, in order to murmur abject nonsense and interject confessions that acquire the tone of a short prayer or a litany of insults. Other times, it contents itself with offering fragments of memories, images, and words that appear to have been selected with the sole aim of adding anxiety to his rumination of pointless matters, the private clichés he will come back to later, repeatedly analyzing their limited meaning, like someone rolling a pebble around in their hand. The succubus may spend the day under the bed, dozing among the fluff and dust, or behind the wardrobe, or under the sofa, but the man knows that come evening, it will still be in the bedroom, breathing noiselessly, and he doesn't worry about it anymore or get alarmed; he's come to accept it as one accepts an inheritance, good or bad, or a family defect.

The man links his wife's words to the devastating feminine sincerity she would employ at critical moments, when he was incapable of making a decision. Ana would raise abrupt palisades against the inevitable—definitive gestures, rapid distraction techniques that, far from lessening the pain, brought it back with renewed vigor. That's what happened on the night when, with an almost supernatural gaze, she confronted the young surgeon in the intensive care unit. He recalls the sequence of prior events as a succession of gestures whose final meaning he would never understand—him lifting the receiver, placing it against his ear, while on the other end of the line, a male voice trained in giving bad news—correct, prudent, gently imperative, well modulated—declared that his daughter had suffered a car accident. He held the receiver, pressing it very hard against his ear while listening to the voice, which explained, without going into detail, that Laura's red car had gone under a truck, it had happened an hour earlier, on the brow of a hill a few miles from the ski resort. He relaxed the tension in his fingers and changed ears when the voice, with a demonstration of prosody worthy of a better cause, indicated that an ambulance had taken her to the city hospital. Without understanding very well something to do with a team of firefighters and the difficulty of the rescue operation, he jotted down the name of the medical center. He looked around in search of his cigarettes, then the keys to his car, but the voice, guessing his intention, asked him to remain calm, Laura was in good hands, all means had been placed at her disposal, so there was nothing he could do right now except drive carefully, without haste but without delay, to the city, where he should head to the medical center's intensive care unit. He thanked him and very slowly detached the receiver from his ear. Ana watched him with a strange smile on her lips, pale, very still behind the preparations for the Christmas Eve dinner. Under the champagne-colored light, she asked if something bad had happened. "Laura," he said, avoiding his wife's eyes, "has been in a car accident," and his gaze followed the figure of the cleaning lady who was busy poaching the lobsters for the dinner and now turned toward him, biting a finger, and he added, "it seems it's serious," and Ana stifled a scream. They got their coats. "Let my brother Óscar know," he said before closing the door, and the woman nodded, still fingering her apron with hands red from the heat of the stove on which the lobsters were boiling.

In the car, Ana recalled that Laura had arranged to meet her friends Sandra and Claudia after dinner. Young people nowadays, she reflected, are in the habit of going out to have fun on Christmas Eve, perhaps she should inform them, tell them not to worry, but he focused on the road, the slightly spectral light of the fog lamps, while calculating that the journey to the hospital could be completed in under seventy-five minutes, so while he kept his foot on the accelerator and asked Ana to light him a cigarette, he imagined he could see the objects for the Christmas celebration on the table, the cutlery, the amber light of the lampshades, and the voice of Frank Sinatra, *New York, New York*, cradling an atmosphere he now imagined as sunk in spacious desolation, dropped noiselessly on top of the room, like a sheet, and this descent must be reflected in the glittery baubles and the wrapped presents they'd left piled at the foot of the Christmas tree, but all of this was being swallowed up by the mist, as if these details already belonged to a faraway world, while they advanced without talking, and this impression of now unreachable distance became more obvious when Ana tuned into a radio station playing music, a Bach fugue, and even more so when they left the mountain pass behind them and reached the first houses of the city. When they entered the hospital parking lot, he turned off the radio, looked at his watch, and said, "Seventy-two minutes," as if the fact of having reached the entrance to the hospital in seventy-two minutes, not a minute more, not a minute less, was a margin, an argument that could be used in support of Laura's cause, but Ana, out of the car by now, looked at him without seeing him, and he followed her clumsily, her fur coat in his hand, trying to place it on her shoulders in a vain gesture of politeness, first while they were walking over the icy asphalt of the parking lot, then in the corridors of the hospital.

He believes he felt something akin to compassion, at least for a few moments, when the doctor mumbled excuses adorned with incomprehensible medical jargon in order to conclude that the serious injuries sustained by Laura in the accident were "incompatible with life" and he was very sorry, really and truly. He wondered what this nonsense meant, while at the same time shifting his gaze between the surgeon's flustered face and, he wasn't quite sure why, the cellulose mask he wore crumpled under his chin, drawn by the elastic bands that stretched across his jaw, trapping his ears, like the elastic bands of a child's mask. He remembers he managed to shake off this absurd fascination and, still having found no answer to his question, raised his eyes back to the now silent face of the doctor, who remained standing opposite them with drooping arms, as if considering the effect produced by his words. This interval of silence, however, was very short, for Ana hurried to break it. "Get out of here, leave us alone, please," she said with a forcefulness that days later, when he recalled the scene, he judged to be incoherent. Perhaps she, too, had failed to comprehend the significance of the medical euphemism and that's why she expressed herself with a coldness inappropriate for the situation. Or perhaps not. He doesn't know, nor can he ever, but he remembers it as though he were a spectator observing the scene reflected in a pane of glass—his wife's profile and, opposite it, the surgeon's green apron, spattered with drops of dried blood, both reflected in the window of the ICU, which was screened by slatted blinds behind which Laura lay dying, surrounded by a useless mesh of tubes, saline bags, and artificial respirators; the silhouette of Ana with her index finger bent in the direction of the surgeon's mask as she said "get out of here, leave us alone." But he doesn't recall the doctor's reaction; perhaps he attempted to mutter a less laconic apology, or awkwardly formulated an explanation as to the importance an organ donation could have at that time, that must have been it, which is why she pushed the piece of paper away and, pointing at his cellulose mask, said "leave us alone and get out of here." He was the one who, with bureaucratic automatism, signed the documents held out to him, the authorization for the extraction of Laura's organs, which for a moment appeared in his mind as still-living objects, pieces of a lizard's tail jumping around and moving off to hide in anonymous cracks and warm fissures, and scratched his signature at the bottom of the documents, then shook the doctor's hand, which felt as fragile as a bird's foot, though he couldn't be sure about this, it may only have been a false impression within the sequence of events; in the next few days he shook lots of different hands—soft, invertebrate hands, arid, stubborn hands, damp hands, icy hands, invisible hands of smoke. He then watched the doctor disappear behind a tuft of blond hair, while he embraced his wife, still not understanding, aware of her suddenly soft body that felt limp in his arms, and her voice repeating in his ear, "Oh, please . . . oh, please . . . oh, please."

In fact, he didn't understand anything. He had a memory of tobacco-colored stones and plaster guardian angels. He retained the impression of air on the back of his neck, and a few faces, not many—that of his brother, Óscar, swollen behind ample aviator sunglasses, the weight of his hand on his shoulder, though they didn't say anything to each other, alongside other, equally contorted faces turned toward Ana. He told himself he had to protect her, but he couldn't, because at the same time, he had to make an effort to stop those same faces arousing his own pain, which, since the start of the day, had remained anaesthetized beneath his coat. He managed it until he felt a cold sweat descending from the nape of his neck to his tailbone, followed by a wave of nausea and the unstoppable reflux of a watery soup of María Fontaneda cookies, very strong coffee, and black kiwi seeds. He moved away from the group of mourners and vomited into a rosebush. He was given a bottle of water and forced to swallow a pill as he sat on the stone edge of something. Somebody fanned him. It occurred to him that this made no sense, was ridiculous—nobody has a fan in December, with that cold frosting the glass of the bottles on the walls and the windows of the cars parked at the entrance to the cemetery, but a woman, the cleaning lady, was fanning him, and he started to feel better. He felt his buttocks frozen on the stone lip. The bitter taste of bile disappeared, and everything returned to a very pleasant evaluative neutrality. He remembers when the burial finished, he even came up with a few words of consolation for a pimple-faced girl that was crying while gripping the railings at the entrance. "Go home," he said, trying to prize her fingers off the iron bars. And he remembers Óscar's terribly pale face behind the sunglasses as he rocked back and forth, his feet very close together, in the corridor of the funeral home, concentrating on the toes of his garnet-colored moccasins, his arms weak and drooping. How strange it all is, he thought to himself, because everything was happening with stunned slowness after seeing so many familiar faces, one after the other, and trying out different ways of offering and receiving condolences—a squeeze to the arm, pursed lips—not knowing what to say, because, to be honest, there wasn't much to say, or perhaps there was, there was so much to say and no way of doing so that it involved a gesture that expressed impotence, disbelief, and pain all at the same time, though the result of such expressive willfulness ended up being more of a dumb gesture—a disconcerting grimace and vague smile.

He wished it could all be over as soon as possible and nodded in response to every polite formula or expression of condolence, hidden behind Ana, swallowing saliva constantly but without managing to get rid of the ball bearing that had been stuck in his throat since the morning and wouldn't dissolve, even though he sucked on violet-flavored candies, until the two of them were back home alone again in the evening. Ana ran herself a hot bath, and he smoked on the porch by himself, the cat on his lap. It was raining, and the water melted a convex layer of ice that covered the garden. The hydrangeas were frozen, and Polanski purred continuously on his stomach. From above came the sound of the water tank, and the faucet filling the bath. Only then did he cry at length, minutely and without respite.

And yet when Ana declared she was leaving, there was nothing, no scenes or weeping, and although he was tempted to give free rein to the actors studio he'd always sensed inside himself, hidden beneath his jacket, ready to reveal his long-suppressed dramatic vocation, he managed to restrain himself in time, and this effort at self-restraint still fills him with satisfaction. Although he barely managed to suppress a slight gesture of horror, he didn't give way to the recourse of overacting; he did, however, stare at his wife in some alarm at the allusion to their daughter, a recourse he judged to be as deceitful as it was effective in the situation, which he also managed to exploit by introducing just the right amount of drama. Otherwise he wouldn't have been able to conceal his relief, since when all was said and done, his wife had just demolished the partition wall he himself had been eroding day after day, and in her words, which she considered forthright and perhaps even original, he glimpsed a kind of long-awaited liberation. The fissures were finally giving way, sending cracks up and down the building. So the sudden feeling of vertigo in the pit of his stomach was a physiological reaction that responded more to the certainty that something long desired was finally happening than to any innocent declaration of marital breakup. After all, everything was reaching the point he himself had foreseen, evidence that strengthened him in a conviction he'd assumed with everyday cynicism and according to which he was a sentimental man, bad and sentimental, which was based on irrefutable proof— his uncanny ability to get somebody else to do for him what he would never have dared to put into practice on his own, to exhaust the options open to his opponent until finally forcing them to make a decision they, in their ingenuity, believed to be the fruit of their own free will but which was in fact nothing more than the logical conclusion of a long-drawn-out and well-planned siege. Victory through attrition, exhaustion, a process in which time loses all consistency and his opponent's intellectual capability is reduced, since once the final maneuvers— prolonged silences, moderate but well-aimed reproaches, false compassion, reconciliation, hurried intercourse, and back to the beginning—have been exhausted, the other loses the match in the false belief that they have won it. This is why, when his wife said "we're finished and you know it," his innate dramatic vocation contented itself with a slight, episcopal nodding of the head—"You're right, Ana, you've taken the words right out of my mouth."

2

The succubus laughs from the bedhead, and its laugh sounds feeble, asthmatic. The man sits up in bed as if that simple gesture were enough to stop the chatter. He says, "Enough," and the word elbows its way through his mind. He says "enough" again and drinks down the glass of water that sits covered in bubbles. He holds the tepid, soft water in his mouth and gets out of bed, ready to spit it out in the bathroom. The succubus stifles its laughter and adopts the pose of a sentimental harlequin. It sheds a fake tear while watching the man head off in the direction of the bathroom, his cheeks full of water.

Two slippers trailing along the hallway, a raucous piss in the toilet bowl, the water cascading down the drainpipe behind the kitchen wall, the forked hiss of the water tank . . . The house awakes with a sudden, vulgar succession of noises, and the anonymous observer slowly turns away from the photographs, leaves the entryway, and moves noiselessly across the living room to the back of the blue sofa at the foot of the stairs. Meanwhile, in the garden, the movement of the cat's ears indicates it is uncertain whether to remain at its observation post, waiting for the mole to make up its mind to leave its tunnel, or to return to the porch and mew at the window, since the man, like every afternoon at this time, will exit the bathroom, come down to the kitchen, and open the door to the refrigerator, that olfactory paradise that promises first-rate slices of boiled ham to which, if the cat is lucky, its owner will add a gelatinous ration of braised chicken and vegetables. The man descends the stairs with a rhythmical clacking and reaches the first landing. He looks much older than in the photograph, an impression that is heightened by a set of clothes the observer would judge more suitable for a tramp were it not for the fact that the house discredits this hypothesis—a frayed bathrobe knotted loosely beneath his belly, coffee stains on the sleeves, prison underwear, the ampleness of which reveals the wearer has lived through less meager moments, pea-green socks that stylize the anorexic thinness of his calves even more, and warped slippers. The man crosses the living room and opens the window to the garden. Driven by the certainty of a snack offered in the form of a wafer-thin slice of ham that banishes the mole and the remote possibilities it represents as a hunting trophy to the depths of an inhospitable gallery, the cat abandons the deckchair and, with feline cynicism, deploys all the signs that indicate familiarity and welcome. It rubs itself against his calves, swishes its tail. "Hello, fucking Polanski," says the man, patting it on the head, while the cat ignores this offensive greeting and effectuates a frail mew, slightly shriller than normal. Man and cat zigzag, getting in each other's way, toward the kitchen. The animal gives the anonymous observer a mineral, transparent look. It is far too busy weighing up the possibilities of slices wrapped in silver foil to devote its attention to the intruder, who is, anyhow, as insipid and odorless as the figures its owner gazes at for hours while lying in front of the television. He may vacillate between going up to the second and third floors of the house, to where the attic is, and collapsing on the sofa, or between remaining at the bottom of the stairs and molding himself to the white cavity of the sculpture in the form of an ostrich egg, but in the end, the anonymous observer slips into the shadow of the entryway closet, into the smell of the elements exuded by the black coat on a hanger, a remnant of dampness clinging to the cloth that retains the suggestion of an overcast afternoon and the footsteps of the man out on the street one Friday a year before, sweating despite the cold, his temples soaked, on his way back home after a week of intense work that had borne its fruit—two reviews for the paper's art supplement; a foreword he'd agreed to write for the catalog of a sculptor; and the promise of a series of conferences as part of the Museum of Contemporary Art's next season. What's more, that Friday evening, having imparted his final class at the university, he'd dropped in at a cocktail party given by an artist presenting his latest video installation. In the natural habitat of critics—a diverse group of well-dressed, elegant people— he felt uncomfortable, but the maintenance of this distance, real or imaginary, safeguarded his reputation as a severe, somewhat anachronistic man. He arched his eyebrows into the distance by way of greeting and made his way over to a tray of champagne flutes in order to focus on the cones of bubbles in their interiors, which freed him from the obligation of having to undertake a conversation of uncertain trajectory, zigzagging between courtesy, preventive flattery, and dissimulation, in particular after the second or third glass, when the bubbles rising to the surface converged in the very center of the glass and the voices and laughter also seemed to mount toward the ceiling. Engrossed in the prodigy of the bubbles, he avoided all commitments, though he could hear the tinkling of the artists as they bumped into each other like the ice cubes in their whiskey glasses. Far from lessening his tiredness, the fourth champagne cocktail convinced him that social marathons left him feeling exhausted, so he grabbed another glass of champagne as it made its way past—it may have been the fifth, or the sixth at this point—and downed it at lightning speed while blindly nodding and shaking his head at a video artist's observations. He then winked an eye at a journalist—or she may have winked a breast at him, he couldn't be sure—and took French leave, slipping off toward the exit. From a distance, his progress through the city resembles an escape more than a walk, a kind of aimless evasion, since his current preoccupations were already a vague premonition announced by slight failings—fatigue in the middle of the afternoon, confusion and doubt, resentment—or with transparent, physical clarity—palpitations, cramping in his calves, dryness in his mouth—unequivocal signs that something wasn't working as it was supposed to, which was something he refused to accept, out of fear, pride, or both, despite the fact that in some region of his more primitive brain, a warning light had been flashing for quite some time. He was overcome by the impression that his body was an added volume, restrained by a weight that had refused to keep up with the ever more pressing rhythm of his mind. He dragged his own reflection along past shop windows, but never achieved unity between his body and his reflection. The most trivial activity—a phone call, a task at the university, the routine preparation of a class—constituted an effort that made this bilocation even more obvious; he looked and saw himself without being able to observe himself completely. This is how he remembered himself in his final class, standing up on the platform, the place from which he measured himself against the slide of a painting by J. M. W. Turner—a man seated behind a wooden table, sometimes standing up or taking a few short steps, glancing from time to time at the script for the day's lesson and the heads of students raised toward him, looking at him without seeing him and listening without hearing him, a man who lengthens his sentences, moving around concepts that vanish in the air like spirals of smoke, while the whitewashed wall at the far end of the classroom bounces his words back at him, like in a game of *pelota*, and the words return to that professor who is explaining the basics of Turner's painting and pointing on the screen to the sky's hesitant line, because "in that fog pierced by light, in that cleverly anarchic disposition of the misty, weightless atmosphere—please pay attention," he says emphatically, heavily, "can be appreciated the ability of a painter to reflect worlds never seen before," he insists, though he knows he is not in a position to offer the excess of dramatic energy required to communicate amazement, even though this also means accepting his own defeat from the outset, entering the classroom with smugness and without hope, because amazement in art is an incommunicable event and there are no synonyms for such a revelation. Clinging to this decalogue that disguises as sublime affectation what is nothing more than pure physical and intellectual decadence, he attempts to prevent his voice from trailing away in a gasp, although he cannot help a drop of sweat sliding down his side from his armpit to his hip, because he needs a breath of fresh air and would run away were it not for the fact that, sheltered in the darkness, he has asked his students to observe the painting, so that half a minute later he is able to control his breathing and improvise a few words in praise of the spirit of the twentieth-century avant-garde movements, followed by a eulogy on knowledge as the only way to attain personal autonomy, but his enthusiasm wanes little by little, and his explanation is confused and disappointing, even for the unconditional female student blinking in the first row, blinking just as the little, voluptuous, clear-eyed girl who gazes at him with her small hands under her chin because she possibly understands, or possibly doesn't, it's impossible to tell, blinks; and in the first row, the ugly, shrill-voiced girl whose predictable questions provoke contemptuous remarks from her classmates and who seems to look at the blackboard as if he were made of clear glass, blinks; and the pupil occupying the far end of the classroom, ensconced in one corner, tall, with hair dyed platinum blond, disdainful, who never takes notes and only listens, or perhaps doesn't, but always smiles, because the girl sitting next to him may be taking notes on his behalf, blinks; and the slim girl who wears stretch garments and violet eye shadow and sits next to the obese boy with glistening skin, slow and efficacious, who bites his nails down to the quick and at the end of class will come to ask him for bibliographical references on the topic, blinks; and the mature woman who is permanently circumscribed within her own atmosphere of silence, blinks. Most, he thinks, are faces without much history, without knots, faces of terse and possibly untamed ingenuity, but he is still perturbed by the fact there are also sad faces that foretoken a shadow of distrust, or a kind of very ancient melancholy, and he wonders where such a premature imbalance comes from; perhaps it should be sought in prenatal experience, in the amniotic sac, or even further back, in the DNA chain, and it pleases and disturbs him to notice these signs of some very young but already ephemeral energy. Then the impression that it was really somebody else who had spoken and gesticulated for ninety minutes would persist, something he realized every time he finished class and gathered his notes, his keys, and his wallet, and there at the back of the classroom was the whitewashed wall, which kept him up in the air, as if his words and movements remained there, floating in the uncertainty of the shadows.

Having reached the limit of a certain critical mass, he felt his insides were experiencing minute deflagrations, cellular displacements, molecular storms that became more obvious at night. He felt he was a syncopated man, because the impression came and went, and when it left, without warning, he would forget his body and regain his natural lightness. But that evening, after the cocktail party, he again felt his body was not indifferent to the law of gravity but rather could be said to be the very object of gravitational attraction itself. That may have been why he walked more quickly than usual, his eyes fixed on the pavement, though still unable to avoid the dog shit and dirty puddles. He heard it from his brother, Óscar, who was trying out a new zoom on his resplendent Nikon camera that day and after a Sunday outing had forced him to pose next to his wife and daughter on the outdoor dining patio of a restaurant and say *cheese* in unison. They returned to the city, and the two of them spontaneously decided to leave his family at home and go off on their own, unexpectedly united by a kind of brotherly complicity they rarely succumbed to, perhaps as a result of a lack of habit due to the strange and radical suspicion every family relationship seems to require. Having knocked back several drinks in a bar chosen at random and lost his composure and the ability to see straight, Óscar, glassy-eyed, said, "You have to realize, Gabriel, maturity doesn't exist; it's tiredness. That's all." To which he didn't know what to reply. He smiled drunkenly, clinging to his stool, allowing himself to be carried along by his natural inclination toward consensus and therefore accepting, with his customary false meekness, Óscar's abusive, existential, and clearly alcoholic statement. He felt, however, that his brother's words were an absolution. He'd awkwardly explained his apprehensions, the insurmountable distance with Ana, the intimate dislocation of one who feels out of place at the age of fifty because he seems unable to find a comfortable fit at work, at home, or anywhere else. That impression of foreignness and intimate duplicity. But all of this, according to Óscar, was just tiredness, sheer tiredness, and nothing else.

He continued walking, the champagne and cigarette smoke banging against the insides of his eyelids, and the symptoms of his intimate dysfunction took on the appearance of an irresistible need to escape, which is why he walked quickly, stepping in dog doo and puddles. Driven by a traveler's urgency, he obeyed the childish lure of the green, neon sign of a diner—the Chipre 97—and entered for no good reason and ordered an incoherent cup of linden blossom tea served to him by a waiter in a naval officer's uniform. He burned his tongue, lit a cigarette, and stared at two women with violet hair who were silently wolfing down pancakes with syrup. On a television with no sound, the weatherman was pointing to some isobars looped like geological folds over the city. He stayed like this for a good while—the waiter facing him, standing at attention against a background of a photograph of a sunset in Cyprus, the violet-haired women enclosed in an atmosphere of noisy deglutition—until the tea had cooled down a bit. He was grateful to have finished work—the classes, the newspaper reviews, the text for a catalog. He imagined the reactions his reviews would have the following week, the suspicions and wounded pride of the artists, most of whom, he thought, were functional illiterates incapable of threading together a coherent discourse. Artists babbled, that was all they could do, and with that false modesty they displayed their works, masquerades, conceptual rags, sophisticated technological monstrosities, puerile games no more interesting than the newspaper crossword. He knew he stood outside current thinking, and this pleased him. Someone had to occupy the place of incorruptible academic, although at times, it was only fair to admit, he had to make exceptions. To tell the truth, he had written the review quite quickly, after a phone call from the director of the Museum of Contemporary Art. The director had asked him as a personal favor, as a way of promoting his nephew, an artist whose sculptures had the curious tendency of adopting forms that were very similar to the remains of planes after a crash. He drew up a text whose vacuity remained hidden beneath a series of rhetorical flourishes that served to increase the emotional heat of the analysis, as if these pieces of metal that appeared to have been pulled from the guts of a tractor really did speak of fear and weren't just simulacra, fragments, pedantic claptrap. That said, the text would guarantee his participation in the major roundtables the Museum of Contemporary Art was organizing for the following season.

He could have written:

The author's sculptures preserve something of the old eclecticism of the 1980s—the kitsch, the irony, the appropriation of traditional icons, and a certain theatrical and hence postmodern baroque appearance in the lines, but the way they have been put together—and the final result, therefore—comes across as an imposture. Yes, the works were executed very carefully, but in the end, the collection on view suffers from the absence of any firm base of support and descends into a mass of aesthetic contradictions. Something similar occurs, ma non troppo, with positioning of the sculptures in the hall. Here is another salient point that does not resolve but heightens the preceding chaos. Some of the works seem to hearken back to a different period, on account of both the technique employed and the proposal put forth. There is a stripping down that is much to be appreciated, as if the author did not know how to unite the iconoclastic breath of his sculptures with a more reflective, mature process or without vain, stylistic displays. In this emptying of forms, there is a tension that could shelter a new expressive space where the Logos could really appear. It's just a shame that the author was unable to unite the two ideas and that everything gave way to an aesthetic cocktail of no interest beyond that of its own expressive stammering. In any case, we will not despair and shall await his next exhibition with curiosity. G.A.

But he wrote:

The author's extensive career is backed by a solid commitment to the most transgressive of projects. And yet his work cannot be ascribed to any of those ephemeral currents nurtured by the cultural industry; rather his work is a successor to modernity's riskiest adventures. There is no frivolity here, therefore, or concessions, because his sculptures demonstrate that the artist is conscious that creative work has its roots in personal determination, separate from aesthetic sects, fashions, and calculations of probability. It is delightful to walk past these pieces of iron covered in rust, twisted and arranged with consummate success and effectiveness to extract the maximum degree of openness and significance from the works themselves.

These pieces of engines, these sheets wrinkled like aluminum foil, acquire before the spectator the muteness of a meaning that refuses to be revealed. They are unknown quantities, objects that in their almost metaphysical quietude appear to be waiting, driven away from their surroundings and uses, like aerolites or fragments of satellites. The works' titles admit of no conceptual whims, they are centripetal, self-referential titles, but they are borrowed from a semantic field that hovers on the border between the purest form of nihilism and provocation. And so we offer our most devoted admiration to this collection of iron pieces that serves to confirm something we have suspected for quite a long time—art is not in crisis when there is genius. G.A.

He burned his tongue. The violet-haired women had disappeared, together with the pancakes and syrup. He looked at the steam rising from the kettle and wondered what the hell he was doing in Chipre if, deep down, all he really wanted was to get home, forget his classes, departmental meetings, reviews, conferences, and sleep for ten or twelve hours straight, and so driven once again by an irrepressible sense of urgency, he paid for his drink and, without waiting for the change, went out into the street.

A timid, cold rain was falling, but he couldn't stop sweating. He reached the next roundabout, and then his heart started quivering beneath his jacket for no reason. He sheltered under some eaves and began to mutter, "Laura, Laura, Laura," without paying attention to the figures passing by or the random music produced by the line of cars rushing to leave the city at the end of a Friday. He said "Laura, Laura, Laura" while standing in the middle of the crosswalk, next to the VIPS restaurant and the young beggar woman collecting puppies whose shit he had just stepped in with idiotic precision, and carried on repeating "Laura, Laura, Laura" as he walked across the plaza, past the fountain, which added an unnecessary note of dampness to the evening, until the psalmody of "Laura, Laura, Laura" became incomprehensible, because it divested the name of any reference (face, smile, body), tearing Laura from Laura until she turned into a mantra that suddenly dissolved his anguish—Laura finally reduced to a sound as pure as the banging of a door, a car horn, a jet of water in a fountain; a loop of air, nothing.

"Fucking Polanski," he mutters, seated at the kitchen table opposite a glass of semi-skimmed milk and a column of María Fontaneda cookies stacked high like casino chips.

He lifts the day's newspaper and opens it energetically. The cat chews unenthusiastically on the dried biscuits the man, having shaken the box of Whiskas with gratuitous insistence, has deposited in its plastic bowl. This sound, typical of pet food commercials, has instantly replaced the olfactory image of a slice of boiled ham with a texture of compressed food that will never conquer a palate like the cat's, educated no doubt for greater gustatory heights. It longs for the days when its mistress used to prepare exotic dishes. She would always set aside a taste of things, especially raw seafood—the tail of a prawn, the tender tonsil of a hake—but since she departed, the quality of food has been reduced to a war-economy diet of Whiskas and milk. The biscuits condemn it to chewing noisily, like a homeless dog. "Biscuits for you today, Polanski," says the man with an insidious chuckle while smoothing out the newspaper on the table, and the animal senses in his tone of voice the old rancor of solitary males forced to share the same territory, and in his chuckle the irrefutable proof of an old offence. And so it abandons the Whiskas with a gesture of contempt, shakes a paw, and leaps up onto the kitchen counter, on a level with the man's chest; another jump, this one more calculated, and it reaches the summit of the fridge, a watchtower that affords it a kind of superiority, safe from risks, where it indulges in a superficial toilet befitting of the menu. Through its skin, it can feel the vibrations coming from the insides of the appliance. This hum consoles it. It purrs. Through its eyelids, the man down below is a silhouette doubled over the newspaper, an atmosphere of shadow vibrating in unison with the evening light and the hum of the fridge, something the man does not appear to notice, absorbed as he is in reading the newspaper. Without looking up from the pages, he dips a cookie in the milk and holds it in the air, between his fingers, and half a soggy cookie is on the verge of breaking off and falling onto the floor. The man resembles his own frozen image now, bent over the newspaper, his hand raising the cookie like a baton, as a drop of milk detaches itself, foreshadowing the imminent domestic disaster of a María Fontaneda colliding with the kitchen floor. The cat observes a smile, or at least an amused state of mind, in the silhouette of the observer, who now sits down next to the man. But it closes its eyes and remembers the man staring at the strip of photo-booth pictures his wife had just discovered in

Laura's toiletry bag. Some photos hidden away among pencils, lipsticks, a yellow hair clip, and other cosmetics his daughter was just beginning to use, with, in his opinion, scant skill and excessive daring. He thought it was a strange place to keep photos, or maybe his daughter had taken a portrait of herself in order to try out a new style of makeup. That must have been it, she hid behind the curtains of the booth, the toiletry bag on her lap and her entire range of cosmetics in front of a hand mirror until she was satisfied with the result. She kept the photos in her toiletry bag so that every Friday evening, she could copy the same distribution of eye shadow, mascara, and blush, the model from the photo booth tucked into one corner of the bathroom mirror. He felt a strange disposition, somewhere between curiosity and fear, when Ana picked up the photo strip with the tips of her fingers. His wife came out with a gesture of disgust just like the one she used whenever she discovered one of the offerings Polanski insisted on leaving on the porch as proof of his nocturnal skirmishes—a mouse, a baby bird, or a lizard. She looked at him from the bathroom door with an expression that suggested exasperation, sadness, or simply disgust, a look that seemed in recent months to have occupied not only her eyes but her whole countenance and erased any previous traces, as if the muscles in her face had all agreed at once to forget the facial disposition required to convey affection, laughter, or pleasure. He was afraid Ana would keep the photos, but she put them back, closed the zipper, and hid the Chinese-red toiletry bag in the cabinet in Laura's bathroom, because everything had to remain the same as it was before the night of the accident—the clothes, the sneakers with air cushions in the heels, the alarm clock, the coffee cup with a picture of the Tasmanian Devil, the plastic-wrapped textbooks . . . This obsession with keeping everything in place as though it were some provincial museum, safe from the passage of time, also included the old domestic habit of the lemon-scented air freshener. That's why, every morning, his wife would continue to spray the aerosol, and thousands of particles would float like an ether between the hallway and the room of his dead daughter, a space he always crossed while holding his breath in an attempt to avoid the nauseating invocation of Laura floating in a cloud of lemon air freshener. And in this same fashion, holding his breath, one afternoon when his wife decided to take a break in front of a cinema screen in the city where they were showing "one of Woody Allen's" (the man is unable to differentiate between Woody Allen's movies, they all strike him as the same, "one of Woody Allen's"), he recovered Laura's Chinese-red toiletry bag and carried it up to his study in the attic. He sat down at his desk and lit the halogen lamp. Far from illuminating his daughter's face, which was repeated with slight variations in four passport-sized photos, the fluorescent tube made it look blurred, giving it a cold, flat aura, an impression that was mysteriously enhanced by the sudden barking of the stray dog jumping around outside, on the other side of the garden fence, opposite Polanski. It couldn't have been a fleeting impression, because the ficus with the strong, dusty leaves in a corner of his study also seemed to shrink back for a moment, and encouraged by this semblance of an exhortation, the man undertook the morbid task of a physiognomist, trailing his index finger over Laura's four-times-repeated face—the oval chin, the very white skin, a little too pink around the cheekbones because of the hastily applied makeup, the beauty spot on her cheek, which gave her adolescent face the strange appearance of a woman painted by Toulouse-Lautrec, the medium-length hair the color of dead leaves, the large, catlike eyes displaying a disproportionate sense of expectation lighting up a young face whose features had yet to be defined, a coat that implied an unpleasant winter's afternoon just outside, on the other side of the photo booth curtains. The sequence reproduces Laura's face with only slight variations, but the man, driven by an imperious need to clarify the details, as if the hidden meaning to his daughter's life were encoded in these variations, took care to identify them—a slight turn to the right, another to the left, further to the left in the second-to-last photo, as if she had been practicing in front of the camera to determine the angle that best suited her features. Finally, Laura returned to her initial hieratic state, but on this occasion she allowed herself a half smile that stretched her skin and revealed a dimple in her cheek, under the cabaret woman's beauty spot. His attention was drawn to a detail—her eyes did not match her smile but remained open, frontal, oblivious to the position of her mouth, and here the man thought he glimpsed a lack of symmetry, an imbalance that belied the daring of the half smile, as if she realized that she was simply playing to the gallery and shouldn't accentuate the gesture with a look that might foreshadow a premature death. For this reason, the man concluded, her eyes grew hard, frank and honest, without a hint of fear, in static awe before the camera's final flash.

"Fucking María Fontaneda."

The cat opens its eyes. It didn't hear the soft thud of the cookie meeting the ground, a barely audible splat, but it did hear the voice of the man squatting under the table on all fours, holding the disintegrated cookie in his fingers while wiping the tiles with a wet cloth. It endeavors to remove the particles of Whiskas from its taste buds and replace them with the image of the mole boring through the earth in the garden, the promise of some living, leathery flesh. It guesses everything, with feline exactitude of time, while the humming of the fridge merges with its own purring—the man will sit back down at the kitchen table, turn the pages of the newspaper, and then smoke one of those disgusting black-tobacco cigarettes, the smoke of which will reveal the tubular rays of light coming in through the window. He will spread lotion on his left arm and not look at the clock on the wall, the hands of which stopped at twenty past ten five months ago. He will then squeeze a blue rubber ball for fifteen minutes, drop it onto the floor, and get up from the kitchen table with an autistic's assuredness in order to open the window to the garden. He will only close it when the cat is back from its nocturnal outing, the next morning, but on opening it he will say, by way of farewell, while stroking the cat's back the wrong way, "Come on, Polanski, time for a little exercise."

The moonlight will force it to dilate its pupils. But if the night promises nothing good or the forest air comes wrapped in strange silence—and it will only know this once it jumps off the windowsill and sniffs the night air—it will return before morning without any mole corpses to deposit on the porch, or traces of fights, youthful conceits it no longer gives in to even when the weather would allow it but which have left one ear calloused and a scar on its skull, old wounds it links to the image of a cross-eyed, orange cat whose territory forms a natural border between the ravine and the gas station. It will return home when the sparrows start chirping on the eaves. There are times the window is closed, and then it will knock on the glass with its paw, *tap*, *tap*, *tap*. That's what the girl used to do to make herself heard whenever she was late coming home, she would knock on the kitchen window with her knuckles, *tap*, *tap*, *tap*, until her mother came down to open the front door. Then it will drink water from its plastic bowl and go up to the bedroom to sleep at the man's feet. The succubus will wink, but the cat will ignore it, satisfied at having completed its rounds and marked the surroundings of the house with its diluted, neutered-cat urine—an unaltered timetable that is never broken and must be followed again today, despite the silhouette that is still watching everything without disturbing anything, confused by the light, the shadow, the monotonous, horizontal movement of the eyes of the man reading the newspaper.

He wets the pad of his thumb on the tip of his tongue. Turns the pages anxiously. One might say he is not motivated by the informational content of the news but by the desire to fulfill a certain set, daily ritual. The repetition of actions affords him a primitive sense of security he is aware of but clings to superstitiously. Small goals that open or close circles, petty tasks whose purpose is to shore up his routine, like jotting down notes on small pieces of paper he then sticks to the door of the fridge— things he must buy, things he must do, phone calls he must make: *Visit the university department; Go to the bank; Buy surgical tape; Return Ana's call; Buy boiled ham . . .* To do lists he imposes upon himself and doesn't follow through on, and then scribbles out only to write them again on another sticky note, this time accompanied by asterisks and exclamation marks that make them more pressing and urgent. It is with this same obsessiveness that he now turns the pages of the newspaper. His glance slides over the photograph of an Arab boy posing with his fists on his hips and a Kalashnikov across his chest. He is wearing a soccer jersey. He smiles against the backdrop of an open field covered in rubble and glistening dust. Another article reports that an explosion has seriously wounded a woman walking along a beach. In the same section is a photo of two politicians. From their posture, they appear to be sharing a secret, the younger one, with a long face, bowing his head and the other, with bushy eyebrows and white hair, moving his lips next to his colleague's ear. The man pays no attention to the caption under the photo, drawn by an article on the human genome and the possibility of reproducing organs in the laboratory. For a moment, he imagines a new kidney, the size of a fist, glistening like a stone recently pulled from a river, a dark red pebble, covered in a network of tiny veins, a fruit throbbing inside his abdomen, but the text explains that experiments carried out on laboratory mice will take decades to produce results. He contorts his face at the news that interest rates are due to go down. He can hear the ringing of the phone in the living room and his ex-wife's voice informing him that she has found a buyer for the house, "*a wonderful couple, he's a Catalan architect, she's a yoga teacher, a young couple that's decided to get out of the big city, just what we were looking for; a serious, cultured couple who, according to my lawyer, are very creditworthy, will respect the house and its surroundings, and are expecting their first child, don't you think it's wonderful there will be children in the house again? It'll be like a kind of liberation.*" Or else it may be a retired German couple, "*they loved the place when they came two years ago, on their way to the beaches in the south, but they've decided they'd like to live in the north of Spain, in a house like this, it's not so cold as in Westphalia, and the summers are warm, that's what he told me, a ruddy-complexioned retiree with the strength of an ox, you wouldn't believe how much he reminds me of your father, he even has the same glasses . . . isn't that amazing?*" Or, in the worst-case scenario, the future buyer is a man of independent means, a representative of one of the capital's old families, a hick who will pay in cash and is all set to redo the house and turn it into a papier-mâché replica of a Tennessee mansion, complete with Doric columns, stuccowork, a spiral staircase, and wisterias on the porch. "*My lawyer's ready to draw up the necessary paperwork, all we have to do is make up our minds. We could start by putting up a for-sale sign. What do you think?*"

He wets the pad of his finger with the tip of his tongue. A pilot whale stranded on a beach. A man in a raincoat covers his face with a handkerchief while two seagulls walk along the rotting cetacean's vertebrae. There are footprints in the sand, and a leaden sky. The sports section opens with a lengthy report on the recent European Cup champions. The players shout while perched on the head of a statue. They're wearing the same shirt worn by the Arab boy posing with an assault rifle in the international section, but he forgets this coincidence as soon as he notices he has reached the TV listings: Cartoons at 9:00; Nature documentaries: "Tree-Kangaroos" (Part Two) at 15:00; *Matters of the Heart* at 18:00; Game show at 18:30; Soap opera at 19:30; News at 22:00; *It Happened Here* (Crime Report) at 22:30; Report: *Mothers for Hire* at 23:00; Late-night cinema: *Nosferatu* at 1:30; *Teleshop* at 5:00.

Today he won't watch television, he thinks, today he won't have dinner, and the cat notices from up on the counter that the man won't watch television and won't have dinner, as always when he is due to get up early the next day and go to the clinic. On days like this, he eats little more than an afternoon snack—a piece of fruit, perhaps, a kiwi with excessive vitamin C, or a fat-free yogurt—because a block of anxiety has installed itself in his stomach and seems to be writhing, following the twists and turns of his intestines, as if an exhausted intestinal parasite were making its way through his insides. He doesn't find it easy to explain his symptoms, which is why he simply says "my stomach is sad," and the nephrologist nods without surprise, as if he understood the cause of this sadness destroying his abdomen. He believed this melancholic fatigue was the result of Laura's death, the divorce process, or both things at once, perhaps he had overestimated his strength and was now going into a tailspin, falling into a pit of depression. He decided to go in for a medical checkup following a night when Óscar, visibly drunk after a trip that had taken him to New Zealand to do a photo-essay on urban Maori communities, dragged him to a bar downtown. He wanted to talk to him, to go over his doubts, his romantic conquests, his professional successes, at least that's what he thought in the beginning, though after a couple of drinks it wasn't difficult to detect a trace of nostalgia in their meeting, for a shadow seemed to have come between them, to have occupied the empty stool where they'd left their sheepskin jackets. He didn't want to talk about her, he couldn't talk about her, but Óscar appeared possessed by one of his unstoppable fits of alcoholic verbosity and talked to him without seeing him, over the rim of his glass, searching with his eyes for something that seemed to be scurrying along the bar top, a grimace, a glint in the bottles. "You're like a character from some Gothic novel, shut away up there in your house, I bet you don't even talk to your cat anymore, it was named after a movie director, wasn't it? Or was it a writer? Tarkovsky? Nabokov? What was its name?" he said, ordering another drink from the girl behind the bar. "Look at it like this. You're fifty-two, you have an enviable job, an impressive art collection, and a neutered cat. That's certainly a lot more than I can hope for in another ten years . . . Ten years. What a strange thing time is. When I think about time, I imagine threadbare innerlinings, I don't know, something like a dream. That's the only revolution it would be worth fighting for. The revolution of time. A photographer supposedly freezes moments. To tell the truth, all I freeze are landscapes, outfits, customs, little animals in danger of extinction, traditional costumes, ancestral habits, a collection of full-color photographs, covers for *National Geographic*. That's what I'm paid for, local color and anthropological flavor, I'm no Juan Rulfo or Robert Capa, but I am number one at photographing Bedouins, orchids, seals, and Maoris. That's not nothing. My work forced me to give up accident and crime reporting, coverage of swollen women, Colombian burials, waiting lines outside of police stations, just awful, and become a photographer oxygenated by Nature and adventure trips. But I'm also aware, don't think I'm not, that to take a photograph is to stir up something of death, like the dust that comes off butterfly wings and gets stuck between your fingers. Pure necrophilia."

Óscar framed him with his fingers and winked his eye through the imaginary viewfinder of a camera.

"You should only look through one eye and apply yourself to the vision at the moment the photograph is taken; everything comes down to applying the basic principle of limits. I can photograph a beautiful girl in a field of red flowers, I can photograph the bare feet of that same girl crushing the flowers . . . You have to decide, up or down. Everything else is literature, criticism, deferment. But I'll tell you something, Gabriel, I have never developed my best photographs. All of them have yet to be made. Some images remain stuck to your retina. And when I blink again, one week, two months, three years later, they come loose from my optic nerve, like scales, and with every image that comes loose, I lose a memory. That's fortunate, because it's not easy to forget. In hotel rooms, I leave behind images and scales, like the contact lenses near-sighted people lose in plazas or swimming pools, but there are other images that never come loose, they stay there behind your eyelids, like glow worms. However hard I try to develop them, they remain stuck to the frontal bone, right here, above my eyebrow, but I can feel they are alive, warm, and I wonder what they're expecting me to do with them. I imagine they're the only photographs worth developing. Because, you know what?" he asked, lowering his voice. "A photograph, deep down, is an act of love."

He stopped looking at him through his fingers and arched an eyebrow.

"By the way, Gabriel, have you been to see the doctor? You're very thin, and you look paler than usual. How long has it been since you slept with a woman? That's what you need, a good woman, a good lay. I know a journalist who's a bombshell, I'll introduce you to her. By the way"—he pointed at his empty glass—"one more Bombay Sapphire?"

But it was later, when they were both yielding to the impulses of their drinking spree, and instead of one Óscar there were two, and instead of one Gabriel there were another two, and suddenly there were four guys drinking gin and tonic—not counting the empty stool that was also suddenly duplicated—and laughing, or groaning, or putting their arms around each other's shoulders, precariously balanced on their stools, that one of the two Óscars, it may have been the original, or perhaps just his double, left a fistful of crumpled bills on the counter, buried his red face in his neck, hugged him, and staggering out of the bar, both of them clinging to the door to help them out onto the street, said, "You don't know how much I loved Laura. You have no idea."

Several days later, his anxiety still persisting, he allowed a needle to be stuck into him in a blood draw lab and very diligently filled a jar with a urine sample he handed to the nurse on the other side of the laboratory counter, as if he were serving her a shot of whisky. Later he picked up the results and took them to his general practitioner's office—a complete, exhaustive analysis the doctor either did not want or did not know how to interpret, simply listening to his chest, taking his blood pressure, and asking him, after a moment's hesitation, what color his urine was, whether it was blond like beer, like a sailor, or oily in appearance, olive-green, with shades of sienna or ocher, perhaps accompanied by splashes of blood, or else off-white, perhaps transparent, like water, whether the act of urinating made any white foam or large bubbles, whether he had recently been going to the bathroom less frequently, whether he had noticed a smaller volume of liquid, or his urine was weak, perhaps in the last few months he had felt an itching sensation at the tip of his penis, and in the face of his hesitant answers, the doctor ordered that the analysis be repeated. Two days later, he called the doctor's office and was referred to the nephrology specialist. By this time, doubt and fear were forming a yellow, scented cloud inside his head. Over the days that followed, he scrutinized his urine, counted the times he went to the restroom, filled plastic containers and noted down the amount of liquid, filled small, transparent glasses so he could observe the color of his piss against the light, like an oil taster, and finally resigned himself to the conclusion that there was little difference between the color of his urine and Bezoya mineral water.

The nephrologist's face was illuminated in the semidarkness with an aquatic iridescence. It took him a while to link this effect to the light being emitted by the computer screen. While the doctor compared the results of the lab tests, he glanced around at the shelves in the office, full of books and scientific magazines, the framed medical diploma on the wall, the certificates of attendance at international congresses, and the sporty detail of a bronze sculpture in the shape of a racket, whose pedestal read, "First Padel Tennis Championship, Golf Millennium Club." He cleared his throat, stared at the tips of his shoes, and compared the doctor's hands with his own. He had the impression all doctors had very thin hands, without any hair on their phalanges, and wore repulsive business socks. As if he had read his thoughts, the nephrologist waved his four-colored Bic pen, shuffled the papers, lifted his eyes toward him, and spoke briefly in English.

"Something is moving on."

He lowered his eyes, blinked, and at his gesture of surprise, repeated "something is moving on" in a neutral voice, without any inflection, from the other side of the methacrylate table on whose unblemished surface his slim fingers without any hair on their phalanges were reflected. He felt he was just waking up, as if the expression "something is moving on," pronounced in language-academy English that was a bit stiff and no doubt learned—he thought afterward with a chronic sufferer's resentment—in order to give lectures at international nephrology congresses had acted like a spell, opening an invisible frontier between them, a liquid surface, like the inside of a fishbowl. That's why he immediately felt certain that, having said "something is moving on," the nephrologist and his industrious young man's beard already belonged to a place as near as it was unreachable across the methacrylate table and the screensaver's aquatic light.

He summoned enough energy to uncross his legs, lean over that liquid surface, and ask, "What do you mean, doctor?" His voice sounded a little high-pitched to him.

"Something is moving," said the doctor in Spanish.

He considered looking out of the window and, as if declaiming something in front of an audience, adding, "The clouds, the birds, the cars . . . ?" But he kept quiet.

The doctor pointed at his abdomen with his pen.

"Your kidneys, Mr. . . ," he searched for his name in the report, ". . . Ariz."

"My kidneys are moving?" he looked at his tie, as if he'd just discovered a stain.

The doctor waved his pen around again.

"On the contrary, they are ceasing to work. They are coming to a halt, they are stopping," the doctor raised his hand, as if wanting to reassure him at the same time. "That's what I meant before: something is moving on."

He felt that he understood everything and nothing, that everything was moving and stopping in a dance representing something he couldn't fathom but must have some meaning; his body, and other bodies, his classes, J. M. W. Turner, the yellow color of his tie, Polanski, his latest art review, the hydrangeas he had just pruned in the garden . . . all of it swirled around in his head, forming a puzzle of encoded messages he should have interpreted in time to prevent circumstances bringing him to the point he was at now, seated in front of a doctor who was looking at him with strange haughtiness and saying "something is moving on."

He raised his hands as if to stop a beach ball at chest-height, a gesture that resembled the last line of defense for something to stop or to start moving, he couldn't be sure.

"Why are they moving? I mean, why aren't they moving?"

The doctor sat up straight in his chair, and his trimmed beard was no longer reflected in the glass of the table.

"What I mean is your kidneys are not working. That's the main thing. We're going to repeat all the tests, but you had better get used to the idea you're going to need a new kidney."

He rubbed the small of his back with apprehension.

"I feel fine . . . ," he said.

The doctor swiveled his chair in the direction of the computer. The *click-clicks* of the mouse made the pause more intense.

"Age?" he asked without looking away from the screen.

"Fifty-two."

"Profession?"

"University professor." He hesitated for a moment and added, "And art critic."

"Married?"

"Divorced."

"Children?"

"No."

"Any family history of nephropathy?"

"Not that I'm aware of."

"Diabetes?"

"No."

"High blood pressure?"

"Possibly."

"Smoke?"

"One a day."

"One cigarette?"

"One pack."

"Drink?"

"Occasionally."

The doctor stood up and came around the table.

"Mr. Ariz," he looked at him calmly, "the likeliest outcome is that you will have to undergo dialysis treatment, I don't know if you understand what that means . . . You will be put on a waiting list for a kidney transplant. That's the procedure in these cases. You should know that hundreds of operations like this are performed each year."

The doctor struck him now as very tall. He glimpsed a pair of striped pants under his lab coat. He felt ridiculous, because fear was presenting itself in the guise of a young man with a trimmed beard who wore sport cologne and who, having assured him there could be no doubt as to the diagnosis and written "End-Stage Renal Disease (ESRD), advise immediate dialysis treatment" in his report, would probably go and play a game of padel tennis at the Golf Millennium Club.

He pointed to a gurney.

"Please lie down there."

He felt cold while taking off his clothes. It smelled of bandages and iodine. A nurse appeared at the door, followed by two doctors. The woman's voice sounded imperative. "Get undressed." He felt the blood descending from his head to his toes. He looked at the ceiling. He thought he could see the profile of his figure on the stippled surface, a white stain he must have confused with the doctor's white coat. He was certain his body was getting lighter on the metal stretcher and could float, if he wanted it to, over the table and the pages of the lab results and fly out of the window, limp and weightless, like a beetle, but this impression only lasted until the moment the doctors gathered around the gurney, and then he was invaded by a sense of vulnerability, especially when various slim fingers without any hair on their phalanges began to press on various parts of his abdomen, and the nurse hooked him up to a blood pressure monitor while other fingers wrapped in latex but no doubt without any hair on their phalanges busied themselves at the intersection of his forearm, searching for a green-colored vein the size of a shoelace.

3

He began to live between parentheses. This was the only way he could explain to himself the distance that seemed, from that moment on, to open up between his body and objects, between words and actions. It was as if Gabriel Ariz were no longer Gabriel Ariz but two different Gabriels, one from before and one from now, who did not complement or attract each other in the least; rather, the two Gabriels, on either side of the parenthesis, repelled each other like two like-charged magnetic poles. In this scission, thought failed to find its corresponding expression, the word to name anything successfully; and yet the world carried on being there, while he, feeling impotent between the two Gabriels—the one from before: autonomous, ironic, prudent; the one from now: dependent, held back by the weight of his body—could do nothing to adapt to its pace. It was like watching life through the window of a train. He stretched out his arm and grasped only air, or that's what it felt like when, having recovered from the paralysis his diagnosis had sunk him into, he had to take the necessary steps to be granted indefinite leave. He signed the pieces of paper the head of personnel held out to him from the other side of the glass and completed the procedure with a simplicity and lack of involvement that accorded very well with the distance that seemed to have sprung up between himself and his surroundings. "I'm sorry, Professor Ariz," said the civil servant in a low voice, straightening up in his seat on the other side of the glass, but he smiled, as if these words were not addressed to him but to a body double who had taken over his functions, the Gabriel from now, and the civil servant smiled in turn, feeling sorry for this poor devil signing at the bottom of the form.

He had the false impression he'd attained a certain imperturbability of spirit, a kind of *ataraxia* that never ceased to amaze his acquaintants, though this mask of stoicism was not the product of an ascetic process but of pure anguish. His departmental colleagues received the news with surprise and a measure of commiseration. His daughter's death, his divorce from Ana, and now his own physical indigence painted a dramatic picture for his colleagues, a picture he disliked intensely, but such judgments made it much less likely it wasn't him this was happening to but rather that other guy, the Gabriel from now, behind whom he sheltered and masqueraded as if this projection were a decoy whose purpose was to attract the heap of existential absurdities toward itself and keep him, the real Gabriel, safe from everything, sitting up in the balcony, as though he were just another spectator of the whole melodrama.

All of this was *too unfair*, he went so far as to think in a fit of self-pity. Nobody except for him employed this useless judgment, or others like it, which irritated both

Gabriels, the one from before and the one from now, his colleagues at the university merely forcing a smile before coming out with somber statements that slid over him like tributes paid to a statue. The dean of the department had added, "Some people will be happy, but we'll be here for whatever you need, you know that, Gabriel." It wasn't necessary to be any more explicit; it was well known that his position in the university hierarchy would be rapidly filled by one of the many lecturers waiting for the chance to occupy a vacant chair. So he left the dean's office and prepared to gather his things. He was helped in this task by a PhD student he had taken under his wing, who now watched as his protector exited the stage, abandoning him to the stormy waters of departmental hiring politics. He noticed on the young man's face an expression of sadness and annoyance as he piled books into packing boxes. The days he spent arranging the move and signing bits of paper were a succession of slow-motion images of which he wanted no part, so he decided to avoid ceremonial farewells. The desk attendant helped him put his things inside the trunk of his car. He shook his hand, which was dry and hard, like a chicken's foot, and drove away from the university campus.

Several days later, he had a telephone conversation with Óscar that was cut off due to interference and an almost nonexistent signal. He heard his own voice repeating, like an echo down the line, the phrase "I'm fucked, Óscar," and the voice of his brother speaking in gusts from an SUV crossing a massif in the Andes. He managed to catch that he was doing a photo-essay on the origins of the Maoist group Shining Path, and he tried to explain to him that his kidneys weren't working and he would have to receive dialysis treatment. The conversation was so confused that the words *artificial kidney*, *dialysis*, and *Shining Path* crossed several times, repeated by the echo on the line. "Shining Path?" he asked, just at the moment his brother seemed to have grasped the situation, but then he heard a curse on the other end of the line. Óscar explained that their vehicle had just broken down. The nearest indigenous village was five hours away. He managed to make out something to do with the car's radiator. "It's shitty luck, Gabriel, it's really shitty luck," he said. There was then a silence that resembled the hollow of a tunnel. "I'll be back in Spain in November, as soon as I've shot three rolls of film." It was stupid to try to explain any further, and he concealed his apprehension behind a forced joviality that was designed to keep his own fear at a distance. Which is why he said "I'm fucked, Óscar" and, as a way of toning down the self-pity implicit in the previous statement, added, "we should celebrate." Their roars of laughter could be heard in unison, nervous and strange, until the call was abruptly terminated.

The impression of unreality slowly waned, to be replaced by the certainty of guilt and an imperious need for physical investigation. He had read somewhere, though he couldn't remember where, "During illness, unknown lands come to light." At the time, the sentence had struck him as a lyrical imposture, unless the lands in question were those of his own corporeal geography. Beyond that, there was nothing of interest. He adopted the habits of a retiree. He would trim the hedge in the garden, crumble half a loaf of bread to feed the birds, and then wrap up warm to watch the decline of evening, lying on the chaise longue on the porch. He would observe the slightly oblique autumn sun slowly losing height and stretching its shadow across the crumb-strewn lawn. At such moments, he thought he heard a breath being held somewhere on the other side of the fence, at the forest's edge, but as soon as he seemed to abandon himself to this contemplation and the sky acquired a mint-colored lividness, those "unknown lands" revealed their true dimension, something so close it forced him to stretch on his deck chair and uncross his legs, which were swollen from retaining water. He closed his eyes and concentrated on his body, but glimpsed nothing more than a black box, a dark, rather lightweight volume that appeared to have been deprived of its weight. This initial impression forced him to make an effort at restraint, as if he had to take a step back in order to locate a much earlier point in the geological layers of his own anatomy. "There they are," he thought then. The hollow pieces, the volume and disposition of his internal organs, that map spread out below like an inner city. He could locate the half circumferences of his lungs, two dark segments that offered greater optical possibilities when seen from up close—two arborescent areas harboring unlikely passages through the forest of alveoli. Some were impregnated with tar, like tiny coal veins, delicate bellows mistreated by his tobacco habit. Who knows, he thought, if they would collapse on being touched by a gentle deflagration of carbon monoxide, shrinking away like embers. Further down was the stomach—slow, resentful, ruminant, a bag vulgar brown in color, a long-suffering abdominal cavity, a forever remembering entrail. He could sense his intestinal circumvolutions, a labyrinth growing narrower and wider through a long network of galleries, a tubular heap where poisonous, fetid gases installed themselves from time to time, rising to his chest in the middle of the afternoon with the alarm of pectoral flatulence. "My stomach is sad," he started saying, because he felt it doubling over with a heavy weight toward the waterline of his navel. He didn't like his stomach, let alone his intestines, perhaps because of their resemblance to worms, which at the time were plaguing the garden. During such morbid investigations, he preferred to stop at the liver, so weighty, so autonomous, brilliant, colored crimson red, like a bottle of wine brightened by the light, perfect as a precision instrument, standing firm despite the functional imbalance caused by his kidneys having gone on indefinite strike, despite having filtered a large number and variety of drinks over the past thirty years—poisonous anise liqueurs, merry ciders, earthy pomace brandies, civic beers, unpretentious reds, sugary potions in suspicious hues, mint and strawberry liqueurs, sloe-flavored anisettes, village-brewed spirits with euphoric effects, fulminating demijohns of gin, which he phased out as he began to sit at long tables of refined cutlery at the homes of Ana's friends and relatives and his backside molded itself to the Chair of Aesthetics and Art Theory. The exhibition and gallery openings, book launches, invitations to conferences, and cocktail parties offered him a new alcoholic menu he grew used to as quickly as he dismissed the bitter taste of strong wine—champagnes, cavas, cocktails, vodkas tasting of iced lemon, cognacs aged in fine oak barrels, armagnacs, whiskies tasting of pitch . . . *My liver? Fine, thanks,* he thought, longing for those liqueurs that were now as forbidden to him as Bezoya bottled water. He then moved up to the heart and its percussion of blood, the heart, serious stuff, the size of a bird enclosed in a fist, throbbing between the bars of the ribcage, to the left of the sternum. He descended through the artery, moved through the left ventricle to the center of the muscle where the pulsing started, the beating that on occasion and for no apparent reason would turn into stuttering heartbeats, off beat, a drum roll that grew and pushed against his thoracic cavity, or further up, even, against his frontal sinuses and eyeballs. They were murmurs, arrhythmias, worrying signs that, taken together with cigarettes, a sedentary lifestyle, cholesterol, and his renal deficiency, could, as the doctor had informed him, bring about a collapse. During such afternoons of morbid contemplation, he learned to familiarize himself with these warning signs, going so far as to dream up scenes in which everything began with a feeling of stiffness in his left arm, a pain that spread to his chest and the base of his neck. In the scene, he was watering the hydrangeas, lifting his eyes to the sky, as if seeing it for the first time, with primitive amazement, and suddenly the hose leaped out of his hands and onto the lawn, like a snake, spraying water everywhere, and he staggered and fell to the ground. He could feel the wet grass under his chest and a few droplets on his forehead as he dragged himself in the direction of the phone to call for help, in the presence of Polanski, who gazed at him impassively from the other side of the window. And so he realized he only had time to lie down on his back and observe that strange, beautiful firmament. But these were mere tricks of the imagination, strategies of anxious free time. After a while, he learned to listen to his body and pressed his ear against his skin, filled with a comfortable sense of moral insensitivity.

Through its eyelids, the cat watches the man knead his blackened arm. It can hear the blood flowing under his skin with an electric hum. And the animal is aware, before it happens, that he will push back the chair and stand to face the window that looks out onto the forest. Though parallel, the gazes of the man and of the anonymous observer converge at a particular point on the other side of the garden fence, perhaps at the foot of the yew that grows at the edge of the forest and at nightfall seems to become more somber than usual. The man's gaze remains at the foot of the tree, and the anonymous observer appears to lean against the back of the chair. Beneath his chin, the man's head glistens, his forehead bulging slightly in the shadows, the space between his eyebrows illuminated by the flame of a lighter he has just flicked on to light a cigarette. The man keeps his eyes on the yew, because he has a certain sense of sympathy for this tree, which forms a natural border between the house, the surroundings of the garden, and the forest, that other territory he imagines as being crisscrossed by moles, inhabited by nocturnal birds, though he's never gone inside it, perhaps because he feels a primitive, superstitious respect for the oak forest, so leafy and dark on winter nights. So the yew is the point of division, the marker. The cat's green pupils dilate at the same time as the man extinguishes the flame on the lighter, and the shadow's silhouette seems to protect him, leaning toward him over the crown of his head and the hood of his frayed bathrobe, but the man moves over to the window, opens it, and squints at the triangle formed by the top of the tree and the ground covered in undergrowth, at the shadow that is cast by the yew, or that seems to break away from it and spread with gaseous suavity, leaving the forest, approaching over the lawn, weightless between the orange spotlights. He remains standing at the window, his arms hanging at his sides, in a gesture of incredulity at *that* which seems to fill the light and the branches of the oaks, and he senses an impulse of laughter or mourning rising from his stomach, a gentle convulsion, because, in front of him, there is an undulation of breath. The cat narrows its eyes when it sees the man lean against the window frame, overcome by a fit of sobbing that has nothing to do with sadness, or sorrow, but with an internal crumbling, like the collapse of a wave breaking on the shore of his skin and sweeping away his memory. Leaning against the window frame, his chin resting on his chest, he notices how everything that surrounds him is strange, he perceives the breath of each leaf that has yet to grow on the bare branches, and the breeze that has sprung up, bringing with it the scent of moist earth. There is amazement in his eyes when he observes his hands, and the displaced chair, alone in the semidarkness of the kitchen with the almost metaphysical quietude of an abandoned object, and Polanski purring on top of the fridge. He reaches the chair and falls into it.

The cat discerns a line of shadow from which emanates something akin to a smile, and it closes its eyes again, because *drip, drip, drip*, the bathroom faucet is dripping into the bathtub, each drop crashing onto the ceramic surface, just as the drops of rain, *drip, drip, drip*, crashed against the floor of the porch on the night the woman thought she saw Laura in the hallway.

The cat mewed in the kitchen toward the angle of the stairs. It had just returned from its nocturnal outing and on entering the house noticed a vague smell of fresh-squeezed lemons that spread through the living room and was climbing to the next floor. It followed the trail and caught sight of boots stepping on the stairs without making the floorboards creak, and also the waterproof fabric of a red parka. It mewed even more loudly at the foot of the stairs, until the man awoke in the bedroom and it sensed him feeling around on the still warm sheets with his hand and stepping barefoot into the hall. In a nightdress, outside Laura's bedroom, the woman was observing the shadows of furniture with a sleepwalker's glassy gaze. The man came up to her sleepily, his hair stuck to his forehead and his eyelids swollen.

"What is it?"

"It's Laura," she pointed to the far side of the bedroom.

"What?"

"Laura, it's Laura," she repeated.

"What do you mean?"

The man looked in the direction his wife's finger was pointing. He poked his head inside the bedroom.

"There," she insisted.

He sighed very gently. Put his arm around her.

"Let's go to bed."

"Can't you smell it? Polanski noticed it, too," she said, pointing toward the cat.

"Please, Ana, let's go to bed. There's nothing there."

He took her by the elbow, and the two of them moved off down the hallway. But after they'd gone back to bed, there remained on the second floor the soft scent of wet hair, and the parka fabric, cold, almost frozen, and a trace of defenselessness, which is why it mewed even louder than before. After a while, the man stuck his head out the door, and his face was full of knots, and it was still like this when he raised a slipper in the air and hurled it at the cat. The projectile missed its head by a mere inch and crashed into the wall. As it fled toward the living room, it heard the voice of the man cursing from upstairs. "Fucking Polanski."

4

"In-put, out-put; in-put, out-put . . . ," recites the man in time to the rhythm marked by the machine, apparently indifferent to the loop formed by the two plastic tubes through which his blood is circulating. Dozing in the imitation-leather armchair, "in-put, out-put; in-put, out-put . . . ," he keeps his right hand on his forehead without noticing that, outside, a new day has begun under a weak sun, soft and frosted like the skin of a winter orange. A dirty light pours over the city through the clouds, but the man is unable to see this, since the dialysis room still gives off an impression of night, as if it hadn't dawned yet, and this appearance is due to the light coming from the fluorescent tubes, which radiate the ancient luminosity of a classroom.

It's already after nine. The patients have been connected to the machines for an hour. The voices of the nurses gathered around their coffee in an adjoining room form a distant counterpoint to the soft, monotonous noise of the machines and the sighs and coughs of the patients who are asleep, or listening to the radio with earphones, or doing like the man, who keeps his left arm still on the armrest while mumbling "in-put, out-put; in-put, out-put." Man and machine seem to be connected by a bond far more complex than periodic renal depuration therapy, and though the ties of the transparent plastic tubes that join them might suggest a fragile connection, the truth is that an attitude of iron discipline seems to have sprung up between them, which a routine repeated over the last six months—five hours a day, three days a week—has transformed into a dependence that is familiar, even desirable, but ultimately unhealthy. The man rocks in a relaxed position, like a tourist on the beach, one knee bent, his hip sunk in the reclining chair. He is filled with a sense of complacent lassitude, since he almost can't feel the points of pain in his arm; this morning the jabs were rapid and accurate, with none of the annoying mishaps that rather regularly slow down the venipuncture process in a painful operation of trial and error he generally endures with a stoicism that does not exclude the odd curse muttered under his breath. "Sonofabitch, goddammit," he whispers with a strained expression, pale from the pain, when Sara, the nurse, fiddles with the needles in search of his bloodstream. There is still, however, the inevitable apprehension of a bite, and he imagines the stings of a metallic insect under his skin. This is why he continues saying "in-put, out-put; in-put, out-put" and keeps his arm very still, so that the insect will persist in the attitude of a subcutaneous parasite for the next five hours. For as long as this pact of stillness holds, the blood will keep flowing, gently pumped through the cannula.

The prelude to this is enacted early each morning with monotonous exactitude, without variation, and this repetition of actions appears to have been conceived as a way of molding the patient's will, in terms of both security and fear. The arrival by taxi, stopping at the entrance to the clinic, the wait in a little room next to the elevators, which are decorated with pious, soothing iconography—Millet's *The Angelus*, Fra Angelico's *The Annunciation*—and the shrill notes of an oboe playing "Raindrops Keep Falling On My Head" on a loop over the loudspeakers, a melody he hums to himself as he advances down a hallway whose walls retain a vague aroma of anesthesia, of patients, and everything passes in front of his eyes, still swollen from the fluid retention of the last forty-eight hours, as though it were a dream, and the impression continues in the elevator, because the song keeps playing inside the cabin, above his head, until he stops at the eighth floor. He replies to the greeting muttered by the patients who have been waiting for a while, seated on cretonne sofas in the anteroom, but says good morning so quietly that only his shirt collar hears him, and he walks straight past and pushes open the door, resting his hand on the sign with blue letters that reads, "Dialysis Room. No Entry To Unauthorized Persons."

He got undressed in front of the mirror, and he had the impression the glass did not reflect him but rather a sleepy shadow that appeared to be duplicated behind him. He came out of the cubicle in a pair of beige-colored pajamas and weighed himself on the scales. The ward manager confirmed his excess weight. "Three point seventy-five pounds," she said, while at the same time jotting down the figure in her accountant's notebook. He ignored the nurse's reproachful tone and sat down at the venipuncture table. He rolled up his left sleeve and tied the rubber band around his biceps, using his mouth to help him, like a junkie. Other patients close their eyes, look away, chatter with false joviality, or slip in some meteorological comment, something that in the man's eyes serves only to aggravate the procedure, since nothing will stop Sara sticking two needles as thick as Bic ink cartridges into their arms. Unlike the others, he doesn't look away, he needs to keep an eye on the process, to see how the other nurse's gloved fingers feel for the fistula and choose the exact spot, so that in this rather childish way, he can foresee the intensity of the pain that is coming as soon as Sara sticks in the needles. He then holds his breath, clenches his jaw, and counts to ten. But this morning he got to seven without feeling any pain, the needles having slipped through his skin with silky precision, without a tear. The nurse clamped the tubes and released the rubber band. "All set," she said, and he looked at her without seeing her, surprised by the painless exactitude of the operation. Sara cracked some joke about bullfighting he couldn't quite make out—it may have had something to do with *banderillas* and a scrawny bull—and only then, on his way to his armchair, holding his tubed arm aloft, did he noiselessly expel the air retained in his lungs, all without so much as a "sonofabitch, goddammit."

He only has to wait for the time to pass quickly while his blood enters the machine through the plastic tubes, passing through filters and circumvolutions where it is mixed with saline solutions and cleansing serums whose taste he begins to note on his soft palate—"in-put, out-put; in-put, out-put." Now he knows what to expect, he is familiar with every one of the machine's sounds and their meanings, he can recognize the first symptoms of a blackout, he is aware he might have cramps in his calves at the end of the session, that the needles sometimes come out and have to be reinserted, that the machine might detect an air bubble and halt with a beep of alarm; it's better to sleep, to relax, to become one with the prosthesis that is the machine, not to think too much, or perhaps to think too much, one never knows, until sleep comes or he is overwhelmed by tiredness. He is no longer alarmed at seeing his blood depart from him, not like in the beginning. The first time, six months ago, he couldn't help feeling faint when he saw his dark, poorly oxygenated blood heading in short bursts toward the machine's insides. He stared at this technical feat while sitting paralyzed in the imitation-leather armchair after a nurse with short, muscular legs had shown him in, as if inviting him to take part in a social gathering. There were men and women asleep, connected to their dialyzers by cables. One or two raised their hands in greeting. He felt dizzy. The nurse was not unaware of his weakened spirit, flustered as she was at having given the new patient a smooth, round bruise after several failed attempts to stick the needles in his fragile veins, slippery as snakes, as the ward manager had remarked while watching this young woman's first venipuncture with an examiner's scrutinizing gaze, something the tremulous university professor, despite his dizziness and pain, couldn't help noticing. He reached the armchair, and his forearm felt swollen like a leather ball, but he thought this must be normal, and he clung to this thought as he watched his blood leaving his body for the first time. It was simple and strange—five liters of blood with extremely high levels of urea, phosphorus, and potassium exited his body, passed through filters, saline solutions, and valves, only then to return to the inside of his bloodstream, cleansed now of waste, as pure as water from a mountain spring. It was a simple exchange of fluids, and the process gave him the idea that his insides formed a network of nickel-plated, translucent arteries, the circulatory system of a highly primitive organism. It occurred to him that he had descended on the zoological scale and attained primitive perfection. He had seen this in nature documentaries, primitive organisms are the simplest, the ones that do without any biological ostentation in order to adapt to their environment with a minimum expenditure of energy, and now he was two things—an entry tube and an exit tube. He felt his heart pumping blood and the force of each beat being transmitted to the tubes, which trembled on his arm with the slight, regular quivering of antennae. Apart from his sense of alarm and anxiety, the process could be reduced to something as simple as falling in time with the machine, its gentle, monotonous rattling—"in-put, out-put; in-put, out-put." After half an hour, a woman in a pink-colored uniform brought in a tray with breakfast—coffee, bread, butter, and jam. The woman broke the roll in two and spread butter and jam on both portions. She pointed to the plastic cup, poured in coffee and milk. "Sugar?" she asked. "Two," the man replied, making a *V* for victory with his fingers.

The procedure has been enacted without variation, the nurse has continued spreading jam on the bread, and he has eaten it with one hand in order to then fall asleep next to the machine with his left arm motionless and bread crumbs in the folds of his pajamas. This repetition of actions—five hours, three times a week—has put him in his place, among the other patients occupying other dialyzers—Ángel, dozing next to him with a radio pressed against his ear, dreaming of cakes and swimming pools; Andrés, a Jehovah's witness who, in Ángel's words, approaches his treatment as if he were buying shares in the real estate agency of Heaven; Marcela, a palmist and tarot card reader who has an astrological phone-in show on a local radio station, which envelops her in an aura of mystery, something that, in Andrés's words, the hospital workers compensate for by giving her extra attention; Ambrosio, an ex-miner who drinks and eats with suicidal abandon; and Tere, a small, deaf girl with the face of a tawny owl, whom he has never heard say a word or seen reading anything or listening to the radio, who only ever stares out of the window at the pigeons delousing themselves on the sill, as if she didn't know why she was there, and who on occasion, whenever Sara misses the fistula and a small jet of black blood emerges from the hole, shudders slightly and emits a squeak very similar to the sound of a badly oiled door.

At the start of his treatment, he would become quickly overwhelmed by tiredness and close his eyes, and his brain would activate a superficial sleep that merged with the fermented smell of iodine, disinfectant, and sweat, a fleeting, fragile sleep, like on a bus journey. He dozed, attentive to the slightest movement of his arm. It usually happened that his mind would wander, leaving the room, and at that pleasant distance he would become unaware of his body, to the point that his arm, relaxing, would slip off the armchair. This slight movement was preceded by a sudden feeling of vertigo. He would then wake up, and the fluorescent light from the tubes on the ceiling would flood his abruptly open eyes. The first time, he blinked on feeling a slight tear in his skin. He thought he saw the succubus of his bad dreams climbing toward the lights. He blinked again to push away the steadily growing pain, but his arm kept swelling under the tape like a bladder. The process ground to a halt, and the machine emitted a shrill alarm that shot through the room and the dreams of the other patients, bouncing off the ceiling, against the windows, zigzagging over the tiles, like light from a laser pen, until it reached the nurses' station at the far end of the corridor. He stared in amazement at his swollen arm and the loose needles.

"Oh my . . . ," exclaimed a nurse, heading for the machine. He saw her pressing buttons and clamping tubes. She proceeded to rummage around under the skin of his arm with the needles. It seemed to him she did this with an electrician's fluency. He clenched his jaw when he felt the tiny steel tips digging under his skin and swore under his breath.

"Oh my . . . ," exclaimed the nurse again, continually moving the needles in search of the bloodstream until, finally, the blood went back to circulating through the tubes. She put surgical tape over the wound and wagged her finger, as if telling off a child. "Don't forget to practice with your rubber ball, fifteen minutes a day," she insisted, "you have to strengthen those veins. And as soon as you get home, put some anti-inflammatory cream on that forearm, you're going to get a good bruise."

He watched her head recede toward the nurses' station, her updrawn hair bouncing on the back of her neck, sun-tanned, gymnastic, and was suddenly overwhelmed by an extravagant mix of gratitude and guilt.

He repeats "in-put, out-put; in-put, out-put" in the knowledge that it's not the needles or the machine but he who is living under a parasitic, dependent regime, since the real burden is his body and not the machine, which will always remain focused on the perfect logic of its surroundings, deaf and dumb, oblivious to the fact that he is a man rather than anything else with a circulatory system—a horse, a monkey, a cow. This idea envelops him in a deceptive sense of self-complacency he isn't always capable of avoiding, since it confirms his suspicion that he is living in constant deferment, between parentheses. Once connected to the machine, he only has to worry about the feeling of guilt concerning his blood and the fear of it being wasted as it passes through the tubes. Like all patients, he knows he is under obligation to inspect his own excrescences, not without a certain fearful satisfaction. The machine is running, and he notices every change, every arrhythmia, oblivious to anything not ascribed to that state of siege. In this way, man and machine each continue in their own space.

The doctors have their names embroidered in blue thread and their pockets full of ballpoint pens, felt tip markers, and pencils. The head of the nephrology department is in the habit of squeezing the feet of patients while reading the results of their latest analyses. The others merely nod in silence, knowledgeably, huddled around the ward manager's notebook, and after their rounds, once the director of the nephrology department has squeezed, one by one, the feet of all the patients, they move off down the hallway, forming a hermetic group of healthy, freshly showered men who leave the pleasant aroma of cologne in their wake. He thinks they already constituted a separate group before they entered the room, like all the other men and women not in the hospital—people walking down the street on their way to work, the bus driver charging passengers for their journey, the lottery ticket vendor stationed at the door to the healthcare center—because at heart and in practice they *are* in another place. Or perhaps he's the one who's in another place. This impression of foreignness begins in his body and spreads outward, as if the fact of having a sick body transported him to another sphere of reality and conferred on him the suspicion of a crime. At times, this impression crystallizes and turns into resentment; he catches himself staring at another driver through the window of the taxi, somebody who is smiling or talking to himself while listening to music or going over the day's tasks, stopped at the light, in his car, without realizing that next to him, reclining in the seat of the taxi taking him home or back to the clinic, someone is envious of his healthy complexion, his glistening eyes, his absorption in the music or some banal concern, and for a moment would like to be that carefree driver returning home after a day's work, to take his place, and for that man to suddenly feel the exclusion and the affront of illness and spend five, six years, or possibly the rest of his life, connected to the machine, "in-put, out-put; in-put, out-put."

At times, both Gabriels, the one from before and the one from now, fight to cut each other off in mid-sentence, they contradict each other, and the one from before is unwilling to see himself projected onto that apprehensive, rancorous straw man, while the Gabriel from now attempts to escape from the present moment, drawn by the gravitational force of his body, and tries to project himself onto a future that, like the past, is nothing more than conceited verbiage. This fight was not stopped but exacerbated by Ana's visit, every time he felt the look she gave him, having warned him on the phone she was doing this "only because I want to see you, find out how you are, if you don't mind, of course, it's been ages since we last saw each other, besides I want to discuss some matters of a practical nature that have yet to be settled." He wasn't ecstatic about the idea of his ex-wife seeing him prostrate on the armchair, but decided that the possibility of contemplating her from this perspective would be like watching her through a shop window, buttressed by the prestigious distance of a chronic sufferer. And so he agreed to it. She looked different to him, slim, she was carrying a tiny cowhide handbag over her shoulder, and she entered the room with a lack of inhibition he judged inappropriate for such a place, walking on heels that sounded very thin, *clack, clack, clack*, and produced a series of beats on the tiles. There was no trace in her of sorrow, or of the social manners he presumed should be adopted in this sort of place, rather she appeared more energetic and beautiful than before and, above all, brimming with health. She leaned forward to kiss the air a couple of millimeters away from his cheek and pulled up a stool to a spot near the machine. He neither wanted nor was able to ignore her crossed legs swathed in black tights, or her thick sandalwood perfume, or her eyes, which looked back and forth between him and the machine as if she were in front of two speakers and didn't rightly know which of the two to address, the man or the machine, the Gabriel from before or the one from now. But this moment of doubt lasted barely the time it takes to blink, and her voice sounded deeper, free of hesitant inflections, perfectly adjusted to the meaning of her words, when she said with curious ease, while glancing at the tubes, "The truth is, Gabriel, I imagined it would be worse than this, much worse." The man forced a smile, sat up in the chair, and placed his elbow on the armrest. "You've taken the words right out of my mouth, Ana. That's just what I was going to say. It's all a question of habit." She talked about the house, about lawyers and possible buyers, and the man nodded in an attempt to occupy the masculine place he thought corresponded to him in the matter of the sale of real estate, but his ex-wife talked without looking him in the eye, as if somebody were moving behind him, glancing at the ties of tubes and their rhythmic, antenna-like quivering, taking care to describe all the latest progress, the names of agencies that could handle the paperwork. "Apart from that, I'm doing OK, quite OK, to tell the truth. I don't want to pressure you, but my lawyer is taking care of all the necessary steps and thinks there won't be any problem finding a buyer. We'll do all of this as good friends, you know, without haste but without delay." He nodded, taking pleasure in gazing openly at her lips, but she didn't seem perturbed by his silence. "I don't know how you can still live there, at the house. Something could happen to you, I don't know, an accident or something, and you're all alone . . . why don't you move to the city? I'm sure Óscar could help you find an apartment, a studio, something more in keeping with your situation." He reveled in staring at her lips and maintaining a silence that used to drive her crazy, an old trick that now had no effect. Ana uncrossed her legs and smoothed her skirt. A nurse offered her a glass of water, which she accepted. "How is Polanski?" she asked. He looked at her knees, which were very close together, and her white hands. "Hunting moles," he replied. Ana looked at him over the rim of her white, plastic cup. "The nurses seem very kind," she smiled. The man went through the farce of recovery. He assured her he was feeling better since the treatment began and was comfortable at home, he had more time than ever to read, though he read very little and didn't write at all, he'd stopped reviewing art, at least for the time being, but he went on long walks, took care of the garden; no, he wasn't going stir-crazy, not at all, quite the opposite, in fact he'd never felt so well, though he admitted Ana's proposal was quite sensible, a studio in town would be more than sufficient for him, especially bearing in mind the constant taxi journeys required by his treatment. In town, he might be able to hire a cleaning lady to take care of the housework. Ana gestured sympathetically and consulted her wristwatch. "I don't want to pressure you, just think about it. I only want what's best," she said. He remembers Ana hesitated for a moment on getting up from the stool, blew him a kiss off the palm of her hand, and then her quick steps and her tiny cowhide handbag and the sandalwood perfume disappeared down the tiled corridor.

"In-put, out-put; in-put, out-put . . ." Ángel has spent the whole morning snoring lightly, curled up like a hedgehog. The man stretches his arm out and touches the needles through the surgical tape. He has the impression his body has been emptied on the inside, but at the same time, this impression of emptiness is not incompatible with a sudden heaviness that settles onto his joints, his feet, his eyelids, as if the slightly foul air in the room were an added weight. The hum of the artificial kidney moves away, and he senses his body descending, and there is a dot of light in the middle of his forehead, something subtle, a very fine, luminous pinpoint. He senses that this is where sleep resides, he tries to hold on to it, with superstitious certainty. He almost can't feel the imitation leather of the armchair stuck to his back or the voices of the nurses reciting weights, temperatures, and clinical numbers, and these voices from the adjoining room seem to ease his descent through a camera obscura whose screen he must pass through to keep on going downward. He walks, and there are birds and tabby cats and ravines whose bottoms cannot be seen, because he notices a sound that lends the scene a strange harmony, and this encourages his passage through the entryway of his house, which is now decorated with extravagant surgical motifs—a metal coatrack of saline bags, tubes, and syringes on the porch. Polanski walks among beige-colored pajamas, and the man feels a vengeful impulse, but there's no need to give the cat a kick, because at that precise moment, it disappears with the illusory effect of a magic trick. The man walks through this stage set toward a woman who seems to be waiting for him, naked on the blue sofa, her legs swathed in black tights, and while it looks like his ex-wife, her face does not possess his ex-wife's features, and there comes over the face a strange familiarity that reminds him of Laura, there's a green cloud that smells of freshly squeezed lemons, and she seems not to notice it, all she does is stand up and stroke his arm without smiling, without showing any signs of affection, with a seriousness that seems to search out the depths of his eyes. The man feels a strong desire to touch her, to encircle her naked breasts with his hands, and to rub her nipples, as small and hard as coffee beans, with the tips of his fingers, but the woman withdraws, because there's something running around on the floor. He moves away on feeling himself being bitten by the cat, which clings to his arm and rips the skin with its back paws. An intermittent sound forces its way into his dream. The machine stops, and the dream melts away, and the man wakes up with the light of the fluorescent tubes pouring over his face. Sara tinkers with the machine, and the alarm signal ceases. "A bubble of air, that's all it was," she murmurs, and the man nods, and the machine goes back to working invariably, with the gentle rattling of a watermill. He sighs and closes his eyes, searching for the green mist that smelled of freshly squeezed lemons and for the woman with the black nipples who calmly and resolutely surrendered herself to him, but on this occasion it seems he dreams of going back to teaching at the university, back to attending book launches and roundtables, because it has all been a misunderstanding, and his kidneys are functioning like turbines, two perfect machines that give him back his strength, and he starts writing essays on contemporary art again and rescues himself for a short, dreamlike moment that may only last the time it takes to blink, but that he wishes would last for the fifty minutes of a class in which he explains, with brilliance, with lavish erudition, the aesthetic and conceptual principles of Mark Rothko's meditative painting.

Ángel yawns beside him.

"It's almost one o'clock already," he says, gesturing with his jaw at the clock on the wall.

The midday sun has opened a crack in the clouds, and although it is only lukewarm, the light infuses the streets with an icy clarity. They can hear car horns and the noise of bus engines. In strange harmony, the room rouses itself with yawns and coughs. The nurses start disconnecting the artificial kidneys.

The man's body is a dry sponge, a mass of earth without water. He clicks his tongue. The salty taste of saline fills his mouth. He feels his stomach, which is soaked with sweat, and tries to clean the breadcrumbs

that have stuck to the skin of his chest. Sara fiddles with
the tubes on the machine, and the blood quickly returns
to his body. She pulls the needles out of his forearm. In
her latex-gloved hands, the tubes and needles resemble an
arachnid. Sara chucks it into a surgical waste container or
together with the iodine-soaked bandages. She covers
the wound with gauze. The man stands up, and this
movement releases a stench of grime from his pajamas.
He walks over to the scales as if he were walking on a
glass roof. He weighs himself while holding the cords of
his pajama pants in the air. "One hundred fifty point three
five pounds," says the ward manager.

He drops into a chair. The floor looks whiter than
usual, and something opens in it, a luminous hole he
could, perhaps, disappear through. The little lights shining
like shooting stars indicate that his blood pressure has
gone down a lot, something that seems to pass unnoticed
by Ángel, Tere, the Jehovah's witness, the palmist, and
Ambrosio, who is already smoking a cigarette in the
anteroom, since they have all passed sleepily through
the little lights, a bandage on their arms, drawn by an
irresistible feeling of self-absorption, enclosed in bubbles
of air, heedful of any signs of decline, of their intimate
crumblings, gentle internal deflagrations, oblivious to the
lights accompanying them and the vertigo that seems
now to occupy the whole room and, further off still, the
other side of the hallway. He offers up his arm so they can
take his blood pressure. He decides to wait for the lights
to stop jumping off his forehead. He tests the ground as
if checking the stability of a skylight. He needs to feel
the firmness of the tiles, and that he won't fall through

the hole and disappear like in a conjuring trick. Sara goes with him to the reception area. "Eat something when you get home," she suggests before closing the door.

He drops the pajamas into the laundry basket. The mirror shows him the image of a man with an angular face and enlarged eyes, an odd sketch of himself that looks at him without alarm, without paying attention to the little lights that are jumping off his forehead again and surrounding the space of the cubicle, like firework sparks. He gets dressed, seated on a stool, but the image in the mirror remains standing in front of him, and he has the impression this figure, poised watchfully, will remain there, in the looking-glass, long after he has closed the door to the changing room and turned out the light, heading off down the corridor, with no wish to say *goodbye* or *see you later*, or maybe he will, even though only his shirt collar will hear him, while the notes of "Raindrops Keep Falling On My Head" play over the loudspeakers, a melody he, invisible and stunned, will not hum, driven only by the desire to set foot in the luminous street and feel the cold, midday air coming through the window, reclining in the seat of the taxi taking him home.

5

From the perspective of the black kite flying over the alfalfa field, waiting for a telltale movement in the bushes, the mountains are shaped like a bison's hump, and the clouds, still on the other side of the massif, advance toward the house, the ravine, and the highway tollbooths. The bird's pupils dilate, and the damp earth and the silhouette of a man are reflected in the amber of its irises. His presence may be enough to startle the hare hiding in the bushes, holding its breath, its eyes open, green, inexpressive as grapes. Although it is cold, the day has dawned full of light, combed by a breeze that smells of forest. Nothing presages the storm clouds that by midafternoon will accumulate on the other side of the mountain, driven by the north wind. Like a toy kite flying above the field, the bird draws a semicircle through the transparent air, barely rocks from side to side, folds the tips of its wings, and effortlessly descends in low-level flight. Its silhouette disappears from view. With a gesture of surprise, the man pulls his face away from the binoculars and squints in the direction of the now empty space above the valley floor, beyond the clods of earth shining like ounces of frozen chocolate. He drops the binoculars onto his chest and shades his eyes with his hand. He flashes an involuntary smile against the sunlight. No sign of the black kite.

When he woke up, his body sensed the day's vigor. He stretched under his sheets, ignoring the heavy weight of tiredness and the succubus lazing on the other side of the bed and scratching his calves with the claws of its feet. Taking advantage of a kind of impulse that seemed to come from the forest, or even further off, he threw the blanket onto the floor. He drew back the curtains, and immediately the succubus ran away from the light in search of the fluff piled beneath the wardrobe. He chose not to heed the sobs that sought and then demanded his attention, or the insults proffered in a castrato voice in the midst of a flurry of dust burs. He showered with pleasant urgency, and the water seemed to erase all traces of insomnia. He avoided the gaze of the figure that for days has been watching him shave in front of the mirror. The water from the faucet washed away the gobbets of foam. With strange determination, he tore off the surgical tape, as if this simple act were enough to erase the bruise that has spread during the night over his forearm, with the color of a black plum. When he closed the kitchen window, Polanski descended from the counter and, with a neutered cat's mews, demanded his ration of chicken pellets. He served the cat its breakfast, removing the remains stuck to the inside of the can with a spoon. "Good news, Polanski, chicken and braised vegetables today," he said, depositing the lumps of meat in the plastic bowl with an ice-cream seller's flourish.

He squeezed out the acidic juice of the first oranges of the season while the voice of a radio presenter read out the newspaper headlines: a limpet mine attached to the underside of a car had killed a man on his way to work; the arrival of fifty immigrants on a beach in the south; a hurricane making its way toward the interior of the United States; a politician's most recent declarations—everything gathered together in the space of the kitchen, amid the steam of freshly made coffee and the María Fontaneda cookies stacked high like casino chips on the oilcloth covering the table. But the man couldn't recall the name of the victim of the terrorist attack, or who demanded of the central government an immigration law "befitting of a border country, a host country, as ours should be," somebody had said, or the old-wet-nurse-like name—Bertha, or Lucy, perhaps—of the hurricane threatening to sweep away several small towns in the American Midwest, because he seemed more attentive to the breeze shaping the alfalfa field outside and shaking the last branches of the oak trees than to the monotonous litany being uttered by the radio presenter in a peremptory, urgent voice. While he drank down his coffee, he clung to the idea of a walk. He remembered the nephrologist's advice—"You can go for walks, but don't tire yourself; half an hour a day is more than enough," he said while squeezing his left foot—and the idea of a walk had taken hold of him, and it was a kind of exhortation, like the light framing the forest in the kitchen window at that particular hour with the feigned, falsely autumnal distinction of a Dutch landscape painting.

Seeing him dressed in the old clothes he used for walks, the cat rubbed up against his calves. It may have sensed the traces of aromatic plants still clinging to his corduroy pants, his turtleneck, his jacket, and canvas boots; it fawned even more when it saw him take his father's old cane from the closet and return from the porch with the binoculars hanging around his neck. It watched him, eyes wide open in surprise at this interruption of routine—the predictable reading of the newspaper in the kitchen, the penetrating smell of the anti-inflammatory cream in the bathroom, the slow filling out of the crossword at midmorning—searching in the cupboard, on the sofa, then at the foot of the stairs for the line of shadow it's noticed in the house over the past few days. While adjusting the neck of his jacket, the man said, "Take care of the house, Polanski," and, without further ado, closed the door.

The black kite reappears beyond the space above the alfalfa field. It moves away, taking advantage of a thermal that's forming over the valley at the height of the clouds. He follows it with his gaze until it disappears, effortlessly, on the other side of the pinewood. In deep inhalations, the air brings him the shaded smells of the forest, of spongy earth and trunks coated in moss, and these sensitive signs seem to give rise in his body, which is still swollen under his clothes, to a kind of vigor that is transmitted to his leg muscles and fills his chest with a satisfying sense of plenitude, though the wind also brings strengthening gusts of the stench of waste coming from the direction of the ravine. He leaves the edge of the forest behind. Down below is a drum of detergent, bottle necks, bags of garbage. He throws a stone, which clatters away into rusty machine parts and thistle heads.

From inside the pinewood, on the other side of the highway, he can hear the reports of shotguns, a succession of muffled bangs, like firecrackers being set off underground. He imagines what it must be like to walk from early in the morning alongside dogs following the improbable trail of a specimen across the frosty ground, to be part of a team of hunters that has arrived from the capital and probably stopped at dawn at a roadside café to drink coffee while outside the light of dawn grew stronger, then the silhouettes leaving the cars, rubbing their hands, assembling their shotguns while the dogs frisk about, a group of four or five men that will have fanned out and scoured the pinewood and now, after several hours of exhausting effort, are pointing their guns, because the dogs have finally picked up the scent and bark like crazy when a shadow emerges from the thicket, those men who shoot, as they're doing right now, at a hare that has just jumped out in front of the group and is hit full on by the cone of pellets, frozen in midair, and falls down dead in the bushes; one of them rushes to pick up the specimen, clenches an unlit cigarette butt between his teeth, points toward the cornfield, and says "this big," indicating with his hands the unlikely size of a fox he has seen running in the direction of the highway, and the men step up their goading of the dogs, whose barks can now be heard throughout the whole valley, because if the fox reaches the field, there'll be no chance of catching it.

Another, closer shot does not interrupt his childish entertainment of throwing stones into the ravine to see if he can get them between the joints of a car chassis. In this way, he forgets, or thinks he forgets, the cohort of presences, hums, and voices that seem to accost him at home, from behind the partition walls, among the pictures and everyday objects, in a logomachy whose meaning escapes him and is sometimes confused with the murmur of leaves piling up on the porch, and then other, withered leaves flutter in his memory like dead butterflies.

Unable to sleep, he twisted and turned, and from the space between his eyebrows arose a bubbling of words and the sound of an echo questioning and answering itself, and saying yes and saying no, or perhaps, or may have been, or should have been, or must have been, and his head spun like a carousel with the music of little horses around the chattering and the blah-blah-blah that didn't stop even though he got up from bed and went downstairs, holding on to the walls, and into the kitchen to have a glass of milk and check, while he was at it, if he had left the window open, in case the cat came back from its nocturnal outing and turned up the next morning frozen on the porch. It's better to wander around the house a little to distract the insomnia, to sit in the kitchen and smoke a cigarette, to turn on the radio and listen to the presenter's voice in the distance and some soft music, a jazz composition that jarred against his ears, while staring at the warped toes of his slippers and tapping out the rhythm of the song in the hope that the notes of the piano and the double bass—once he had half opened the window, emptied the glass, and extinguished the cigarette—would encourage him to yawn. He went back to the bedroom without making any noise, on tiptoe, so as not to wake even himself, turned out the light, and the mattress springs creaked beneath his hip, and the soap-pump mechanism concealed behind his forehead turned on, like a telephone answering machine switches on, and again the bubbles emerged from his forehead, *blop, blop, blop,* up to the ceiling, in a litany he already knew he wouldn't be able to calm either by counting sheep or by relaxing his leg muscles, even though he had nothing to do the next day (he remembered he hadn't even put a new sticky note on the door of the fridge with a task waiting to be completed—*Buy boiled ham; Go to the bank; Call Ana*), since he didn't have to get up early to go to the clinic, just sleep, and each attempt to make his body comfortable provoked a new groan from the mattress springs, a harsh sound that struck him as identical to the laughter of the succubus of his bad dreams. When he opened his eyes in the dark, it was almost three in the morning, and freezing outside.

He could have been a man of independent means, a man of leisure, with a healthy complexion, playing golf every Friday morning and improving his handicap from week to week, a collector of bibliographical rarities, a yoga adept who has visited the Dalai Lama and gone around the world three times in first class, someone, in short, whose only concern was to justify time he had bought with ease. Ana's inheritance would have allowed for this and other possibilities, but he rejected the temptation of a life devoted to meticulous, long-winded digestion at the table after a meal at his in-laws' house, of journeys by yacht, in order to pursue his own intellectual goals, which, in the end, had been dreams, only dreams. He needed to avoid naming despair; pathos was the best way to condemn oneself to a kind of ancient puerility, an old prejudice resting on transcendental questions for which there was no answer except a grimace that on occasion would condescend to accept its own melancholy. He needed to avoid naming despair, on penalty of sounding ridiculous, emphatic. "Blessed chitter-chatter that conceals us, so that nobody will suspect we are naked and weak," he thought sometimes with secret cynicism while adjusting the cuffs on his academic robes and walking in time, solemnly, formally, down the aisle of the university auditorium the day the new academic year was inaugurated, *gaudeamus igitur, juvenes dum sumus*; he needed to solemnize the obvious, so that nobody would suspect, to affirm himself without sorrow or glory on the armrest of his position as chair, *post iucundam iuventutem, post molestam senectutem*. Dreams, bad dreams. Language was a wrapping; art, disguised emptiness. A can of air. That had been his imposture, his indigence. Clearly nothing at all to do with real emotion, that material that, in the darkness of the bedroom, he succeeded in evoking in the figure of his father.

He arrived on the first Friday of each month, pulling along the station platform a small case with two changes of clothes inside, a shaving brush, and an ornithology manual. He waited for them in the café, seated at a table in the back, bent over a cup of coffee, his glasses perched on the edge of his nose, adopting a falsely defeated attitude, since back then he still possessed his intellectual faculties, the features of a silent, distrustful character, and a physical strength that was revealed as soon as he saw them coming, when he jumped up from his chair, forgetting his cane, and lifted Laura into the air; a stern man with bushy eyebrows and a strong skull, used to dealing with animals, to sticking his hand up the anuses of mares, to touching cows' uteruses. When he was introduced to Ana, the old man observed her over the top of his glasses with a professional gaze, as if he were evaluating the health of a newly purchased head of cattle, and was able to see through the twenty-year-old with narrow hips and small breasts who drove a car he could never have afforded and to make out a rich girl from the capital, attractive, yes, but simple and squawky as a barnyard bird. He was somebody who had been able to support his family by driving a van around the local valleys and towns, each farm and stable, who managed to win over the normally sullen mountain folk, to prosper, and to provide an education for his two sons—Óscar, so rebellious, such a lover of risk; and Gabriel, so timid, so shy, always with his nose pressed against prints of paintings or in art books, who sometimes led him to wonder whether he hadn't raised a fairy. So when he saw him holding hands with such a refined young lady, he must have thought he was marrying for money, that's right, that's what the old man must have thought, he was marrying for money, not so stupid after all, he must have thought when he saw Ana's expensive dress, her even more expensive convertible, and listened, like someone listening to the rain, to the stories of trips abroad and smelled the rich perfume emanating from that non-existent cleavage and her medium-length, ash-blond hair. He apologized to Ana for his father's rude manners, for the primitive opinions of this provincial man, proud as an Apache Indian, but his father, loyal to his Calvinist work ethic, valuing austerity above any other indicator of virtue, saw in her a frivolous woman who spent her inheritance on trips and decorative objects and filled her time with something so lacking in responsibility and good judgment as writing a book of exotic recipes. He must have weighed his future daughter-in-law against the frugal, self-sacrificing woman who had been his wife, and the result of comparing the two images cannot have favored Ana. He was unfair to her, as he himself had been, and in the darkness of the bedroom, he wondered whether he wasn't condemned to repeat his father's mistakes, though this comparison was also unfair, because his father had made mistakes, but they were honest, born out of conviction, whereas his own had been nothing more than the calculated steps of a bad, sentimental man.

He enjoyed a standard of living he could never have dreamed of with his salary as a university professor and art critic—cruises, social reunions, vacations in inoffensively exotic countries, get-togethers at the house, Art Tatum's piano on the record player, like the parody of a Woody Allen comedy, and he felt very fortunate to be able to talk to a diplomat about Japanese calligraphy, or to a shipowner who explained to him the principles of the Plimsoll line; the good manners, the grateful deportment, the warm brandy, it all formed a pleasant world of soft lights and long banquet tables with mirrors, exclusive places for exclusive people, Ana's friends, her parents, a little false and frivolous, perhaps, artificially cosmopolitan, he thought at the beginning. But Ana was able to take him by the hand and introduce him into this comfortable world with the authentic optimism and lack of pretense of a creature born to be happy. And this, he thought, had been his major sin: to have frustrated the expectations of a being who deserved to be happy, for happiness was what Ana longed for without demanding it, her natural inclination, and that was love, the fact she existed was enough, to glimpse the aura surrounding her ash-blond hair, her white skin, rosy on the corollas of her breasts. Even this splendor would not cease to shine on those occasions when, in gentle rebuke, a smile on her lips, seated on the porch, having listened to his masculine diatribes and taken a sip of green tea, Ana would say, "Gabriel, you men are so childish, so weak . . ."

Ana kept a cautious distance from mundane affairs, placidly, her hand resting on her newly pregnant belly, while showing him the room that was to be Laura's, already prepared, the walls painted a pearly color, the booties, the bottles of baby cologne, the tiny clothes folded up in drawers in the wardrobe, and he inhaled deeply—the fragrance of Nenuco, dry bottom, healthy bottom—kissed her on the forehead, placed his hand on her round belly, and everything was in its place, everything was perfect, especially after the two miscarriages which seemed to his father to confirm his village vet's early diagnosis, irrefutable proof that his daughter-in-law was a sickly, weak creature. He persuaded Ana to buy a piece of land in the middle of nowhere, next to an oak forest, a local road, and an alfalfa field. What better company for a little girl, he adduced, than trees and clean air, walks in the country, less than twenty minutes from the city and downtown, a house for one's whole life, a house to be born, live, and die in, solid, a little solitary, perhaps, but beautiful. And Ana agreed to the plans for their future home.

They were a sight to be seen, seated on the porch or in the living room—his father frowning, Ana praising the dietary excellences of sushi, Óscar already half drunk—and a multitude of exotic dishes his wife had learned in her latest Japanese cooking course spread out before them. His father's face was a sight to be seen, the face of someone who usually devoured rough country stews, now staring over the top of his glasses at an unidentified dish full of raw fish while Óscar made quick work of the wine and came out with the odd dirty joke, made inappropriate remarks, or told some anecdote from his life as an adventure photographer. But it was perfect, he thought, in spite of everything it was, and with the appearance of a ruminant, his father chewed those balls of eel-stuffed rice followed by a dish of strawberries dipped in white chocolate, while looking at Laura over the top of his glasses. In the mornings, he would take her for walks in the local area. He knew the tracks, the forest paths, the toponyms, the names of the different fields, and, when they returned at midday, Laura, as if reciting a multiplication table, would sing out the names of birds they'd spotted—jay, hoopoe, golden oriole, blackbird, coal tit, robin—or newly discovered species of trees and plants—oak, beech, birch, chestnut, fern, lavender, boxwood—words that acquired the consistency of glass in her childlike voice. As a boy, he had also been taught about the diversity of bird life in the local region, and this repetition of actions seemed to him to confirm a bond, that emotional material, which could never be broken.

Three shots ring out in the pinewood like a succession of barks. The sound surprises him as he walks along a muddy path. He stands on tiptoe, but finds nothing strange, here or on the other side of the coppice. He stops to catch his breath at the crest of the path. Further down, the gas station attendant is cleaning the windshield of a car. Jeremías sometimes does odd jobs for the houses in the valley, small domestic tasks that help to top off his salary. He used to buy those violet candies, the ones Laura liked so much, from him. His blue work overalls are too small, he is wearing a cap with earflaps that makes him look like a man from the steppes. Taking his time, he charges the driver for the cost of the service, then hands over the change, extracting a bill from an old, leather money belt. He lifts his chin on seeing the man, aided by a cane, heading in the direction of the river.

He takes a path that slips away from the highway. The sound of engines gradually fades behind him, to be replaced by the wind humming in his ears and zigzagging between the forest and the fields. He likes to walk along the path that leads down to the river; as on other occasions, he gets the impression after a few steps that he is leaving everything behind. There is nothing now to indicate the proximity of the highway, only a wide vista that suddenly appears before his eyes. He is grateful for this emptiness, which startles him and banishes the old taste of violet candies. He advances, unaware of the picture he might offer an anonymous observer adopting the viewpoint of a black kite rising on a thermal—barely a dot, advancing unhurriedly, now stopping for a moment to catch his breath, and moving again, descending, tinier and tinier, almost invisible now, in the direction of the irrigation channel. A happy murmur rushes through the arches of the bridge. He promises himself a cigarette as soon as he reaches the water's edge. He makes his way through the gorse and slowly descends, checking the firmness of the ground with his cane. His boots make a squelching sound as he walks toward the poplars. He chooses a trunk covered in lichen to sit on. He lights a cigarette.

Óscar was a sight to be seen, leading Laura by the hand through the garden, saying "Lo, Lo, Lo," as the child took her first steps; Óscar, the adventurer, who was already crossing the threshold where bachelorhood turns into a habit, evokes in his memory a figure on the grass that smelled of sun-toasted pasture, while the girl, holding his hand, said "Lo, Lo, Lo," and Óscar raised his arms in sign of victory because Laura had just taken her first steps and crossed the entire width of the garden; he looked up from his papers, alerted by his wife's shouts ordering him to come to the window and see how his crazy brother had just taught Laura to walk. When his daughter was no longer a baby but a teenager with a beauty spot on her cheek and eyes the color of dried moss, she continued to get along well with Óscar, as if the fact of having taught her to walk had created an initiation, a complicity. Perhaps she viewed Óscar as an older brother, a mature person who was still immature, or a falsely young adult, someone, in any case, who was not weighed down by social convention, a little harebrained, exempt from the inevitable family rebuke, the deaf and annoying voice of a paternal figure—someone, he thought, as close and complicit and yet as opposed to her father as the negative of a photograph. This special affection for Laura bothered him a little, arousing a father's jealousy he would never have allowed himself to admit, and this bond, which became stronger over the years, disturbed Ana, as well, though they rarely spoke about it, since it was understood she didn't approve of the compliments and endearments they exchanged at family gatherings with an impudence Ana judged inappropriate for a relationship between an uncle and a niece.

He gazes at the embers of the cigarette between his fingers. It could be said that even the murmur of the river prefigures the tone of the voices in his memory. Back then, he was a different person, even the taste of tobacco was different, or seemed to be, and he didn't notice how intense such a trivial act as inhaling tobacco smoke through a filter stuck to the skin of his lips could be, something as amazing as watching the capricious spirals of smoke rising before dissolving in the air, because perhaps in every act our consciousness can dilate and a man can sum up his life in that gesture, a present that dilates, unrelated to words. But he paid no attention to the slightest changes—the air suddenly growing stronger on the other side of the poplar grove, the murmur of the water in the irrigation ditch, the whistle of a goldfinch carried on the breeze, the report of a shotgun—that might encode a devastating, beneficial correspondence. Perhaps that's love. But back then, he was a different Gabriel—a profile absorbed in a mirror, an observer who observes nothing, half asleep, smoking or making love or reading or walking, without smoking or making love or reading or walking, oblivious to the unavoidable fact that the taste of tobacco is bitter and acidic on both sides of the palate and leaves a slight pungency on the tip of the tongue, a remnant of toxicity that inundates his delicate network of veins and arteries, blocking the flow of blood, sinking him into the briefest of limbos early in the morning, after breakfast, over the first coffee of the day and the kiwi cut down the middle and the María Fontaneda cookies, his only concern to feel for a moment the lassitude in his muscles and the irrepressible desire to go to the bathroom on account of the effective laxative effect of nicotine. He would come out of the bathroom with just enough time to brush his teeth and take his leave of Ana, who, together with the cleaning lady, was already preparing some experimental dish. He glanced at Laura's unmade bed, she would be at school by now, and then grabbed his leather wallet, ballpoint pens, keys, and money. He bought the newspaper from Jeremías, parked the car to avoid the foreseeable traffic jam, and approached the university on foot. He cannot recognize himself in that man climbing the steps of the history department and walking down the building's gray, decrepit corridors, which are teeming with students, then greeting the old desk attendant seated like a stuffed saurian in his glass cubicle, just like twenty-five years earlier, reaching the elevator, and opening the door to the department of art history. He could breathe in the air, but he no longer perceived the smell of pencil wood, of old school, that filled the hallway and offices and yet would not escape the notice of an occasional visitor, bringing to mind, perhaps, the combustion of desks and brown paper. This ancient impression is prolonged in the faces that greet him from inside the offices—the faces of interns, some with a PhD student's late blackheads on their forehead, with premature, erudite bald patches, and meritorious bags under their eyes; the forgetful professor emeritus who wears a university badge on the lapel of his herringbone jacket and carries a sheaf of yellow papers, typed on an Olivetti, under his arm; the pointed face of the department secretary, who, seeing him, raises his hand, solicitous and smiling, on the other side of the glass, an unlit pipe between his teeth, a cloth tie and rimless glasses, somewhat overweight for his age; and the distracted gazes of Clara, and Matilde, the latter correcting exams, hidden behind a black mop of hair she flicks back with coquetry, silent and competitive, on seeing him arrive. It is him, this dapper university professor, dressed like an intellectual from one of Woody Allen's movies, walking down the hallway and saying hello in such a low voice that only his shirt collar hears him, and he makes his way to his office, on the polished glass door of which is a piece of paper, stuck with Scotch tape, that says, "Chair of Aesthetics and Art Theory. Professor Dr. Gabriel Ariz. Office Hours: Tuesdays and Thursdays, 10 a.m.–1 p.m."

His marriage deteriorated with the same lentitude with which they used to collect paintings by local artists and invitations to cultural centers in the capital, to book launches, events he threw himself into with a vehemence that could only suggest a certain sense of desolation that should never be named, never mentioned, except in passing, perhaps to exemplify, in his classes, the meaning of expressionist angst, his shadow reflected against a reproduction of *The Scream* by Edvard Munch. He maintained inwardly that such comments were part of the scene, of the embodied drama that a good professor should be—words, gestures, empathy, a certain dramatic quality. And yet his comments on avant-garde art were just a way of distancing himself from the real meaning of that desolate head, those hands covering the ears in order not to hear the inner voices.

He was different back then, he thinks, but he could follow his trail like somebody following a shadow, even if that shadow belongs now to another, just as there are others steering vehicles down a lane on the highway at this very moment, driving peacefully, absorbed in a daily act that, like so many others—having an aperitif, blinking on seeing the first drops of rain, buying a cinema ticket—forms a fragile network of threads, a *maya* of cause and effect on which they walk with the folly of one who is unaware of the void gaping below, sleepwalkers, tightrope walkers, not even suspecting that the thread along which they are sliding at that very moment could break right now—right now—on account of a mechanical failure, a triviality, a broken axle, a flat tire, an oil slick on the road surface, an invisible layer of ice on the brow of the hill, or just a furtive, frightened animal running out of the forest, pursued by the yelps of a pack of hounds that have picked up its scent, a fox emerging from the bushes and racing across the highway in order to reach the poplar grove on the other side, next to the irrigation ditch, and the sudden swerve of the driver who sees only a lengthy shadow, barely bigger than a cat, jumping over the median in front of the car, and the sudden braking of the car, which skids and spins out with a screech of burned rubber, and then the landscape spinning dizzily in front of the driver's eyes, earth and sky inverting their natural order, because the car flips one, two, three times and collides with the median and then breaks the guardrail, and now the driver cannot see anything, or anybody, because the car, transformed into a heap of metal, flies over the hard shoulder and smashes into the hillock next to the alfalfa field, and none of the passengers feels fear, or vertigo, or pain, because they are just silent bodies, three fragile shapes, knocking against the engine casing, the bodywork, and the windows that have burst in an explosion of tiny prisms that sprinkle over the road, next to the useless skid marks and a splash of oil and gasoline. A few objects are left scattered here and there, in slightly absurd quietude, over the road. A flip-flop, a travel bag, a blue and white beach ball that rolls off toward the gas station, and the tires of the car, still turning in the same direction as the wind blowing over the alfalfa field.

That wind, however, carries no sound to the poplar grove where the man breathes peacefully, filling his lungs, only the echoes of other voices.

She suggested, "We could go away for the weekend. The countryside looks beautiful."

And he replied, "Maybe."

"You remember that little hotel on the other side of the valley? What wonderful views it had . . ."

"And a good wine list."

"We could go for a drive and then have dinner in town. Something."

"Something?"

"We should try."

"I suppose so."

"We haven't been on a trip for a long time. I could go to a travel agency tomorrow, I'm told Bali is fantastic."

"Bali?"

"Or New Zealand. It must be an extraordinary country. Or Madagascar."

"The other day, I saw a documentary about some amazing monkeys that live in Madagascar. Although, now that I think about it, I think they may not have been monkeys, but a species of gigantic squirrels."

"I saw an antique shop where they were selling Chinese sculptures at knock-down prices. A real treasure trove."

"We can't fit anything else inside this house. All we need now is to put a terracotta warrior in the garden."

"What if we go to the cinema? Don't you want to see the latest Woody Allen movie? It's just opened."

"All of Woody Allen's movies seem the same to me."

"If you won't come, then I'll go on my own."

"Please, Ana, we're grown-ups here. If you want to go and see Woody Allen's latest piece of trash, then go, but don't make a scene. I'm not in the mood."

"I'm not making a scene . . . I'm expressing myself, that's all, something you never do."

"'I'm expressing myself, that's all,' . . . it sounds like a sentence out of a self-help guide."

"And you? Tell me, what do you think you sound like?"

Their conversations did not end then, as used to happen, with the domestic melodrama of a Mexican ceramic plate smashing on the terrazzo of the porch, or with a punch aimed at the wardrobe door, the same door he had hit on three separate occasions in the same place, above the handle, with so much force and such a lack of precision that, the first time, he had grazed his knuckles on the wood, but ended now without a way forward, with the full stop of the door closing and Ana's car heading in the direction of the city. Anything but mentioning Laura, anything to escape from Laura. So they never discovered a charming hotel or a restaurant whose wine list—not very extensive, but well curated—could have served as a prelude to a reconciliation, then a walk home through the neighborhood, feeling tipsy, searching for each other's skin under their clothes to see if they might find each other that way. They were outbursts, brief flashes of vitality he didn't encourage, since he was convinced that every move Ana made to emerge from the darkness she had sunk into was a false one. And if he did occasionally yield to the proposition of an innocent marital fling, he did so in the knowledge that a Woody Allen movie, dinner at a French restaurant, a vintage wine, and the predictable, fleeting, protocolic intercourse in the bedroom were nothing more than subtle strategies that would make her even more dejected.

Events, however, proved too much for Ana. In the months after Laura's death, she began to lose her mind. One morning, she went so far as to assure him she could hear somebody at night knocking softly with her knuckles, that's what she said—"with her knuckles"— while at the same time imitating the gesture of knocking on the kitchen window, *tap, tap, tap,* and it could only be Laura, that is to say—she explained—Laura's spirit. He tried to convince her that their house was not the house of the spirits, and that the only cause of such poltergeists was Polanski, "the fucking cat," he exclaimed in a fit of temper at Ana's insistence, "going *tap, tap, tap* with its paw every time you leave the kitchen window closed," but Ana regarded him with sadness, her eyes bleary from lack of sleep. How was it possible he couldn't understand that their daughter, transformed into ether after her collision with a frozen-fish truck, wanted to come home? As a way of pacifying the ghost and persuading it to leave the house, he secured the services of a medium from Guipúzcoa. But at the end of that attempt at communication with the great beyond—or the right beside you, one never knows—via a Ouija board on a tall, round table decorated with esoteric liturgy, all he achieved was for Ana to wonder whether she would really end up going crazy. "To start with, I thought it was a mischievous spirit, but now there can be no doubt—it is your daughter," pronounced the medium, still transfixed by the energy with which Laura had, apparently, expressed herself. A few days later, Ana saw, or thought she saw, her daughter in the hallway, in a red parka with her hair covered in frost. That was her own craziness, not his, he thought at the time with a coldness that frightens him a little now and explains his innate inability to give free rein to his own particular ghosts, whether mischievous or not, his intimate energies, his secrets, which was just another way, possibly more neurotic than silent, of dissolving his anguish, since, unlike that of Ana—whose unease kept moving away from her in a kind of continuous exorcism, like an emanation of bad humors, and whose pain was expressed in pointless, compulsive purchases to decorate the house or in cooking new ethnic dishes—his own was a centripetal neurosis, which instead of manifesting itself in anxiety attacks, squeezed up inside him like a ball bearing, locking him in a stunned, hieratic pose. If the plates moved, let them move, he thought; if Ana saw Laura in the hallway, let her take more sedatives; if the cat urinated on the curtains, scratched the sofas, mewed for no good reason in the hallway, or knocked at the window, *tap, tap, tap*, then it would be better for the vet to inject it with a mixture of potassium chloride, or arsenic, or whatever the hell vets use to sacrifice neurotic household pets; if Ana wanted to have another session with the medium from Guipúzcoa, let her do so, better that—he thought—than squandering her fortune on bingo, taking to drink, or ending up on the useless, costly couch of an inevitably pedantic, Argentinian psychoanalyst. Ana's visits to the cemetery turned into a rite she performed alone, one he did not feel part of, though he wasn't excluded, either. He knew they were both creating separate environments in which to dissolve their anguish, private rituals they couldn't share with each other or communicate. They were united by silence. But when Ana asked him to go with her, he felt a superstitious fear, despite his wish to disguise it with a pretext of agnostic prejudice, or a rational argument of distance, or a slight anticlericalism before the liturgy of flowers and priests' high-pitched voices. He thought that perhaps, deep down, what he felt was a great fear of returning to that sacred ground—after all, that's what it was, it was a cemetery—and that the sight of the niche he hadn't visited since the day of the funeral would arouse in him a kind of religious fervor, something like enforced piety. This wasn't entirely improbable, under the effects of mourning, at least. In fact, Ana had discovered in prayer a way of dissolving her anguish, something that in his eyes was respectable, just as the private space he believed he needed, or that he demanded, simultaneously lessening and feeding his pain, should be in hers.

He agreed to go with her that morning, a morning with an overcast sky and a south wind so propitious for migraines and bad tempers. The cemetery wasn't sad but ugly, drab, and crushed beneath a crudely provincial air.

Moss covered the stone of the niche. That's all it was—an enclosed space no bigger than a *pelota* court, with stinging nettles growing inside it. There was glass from beer bottles. He wondered whether these were the remains of a drinking spree; perhaps on Saturday nights young tomb raiders gathered here and held witches' Sabbaths with alcohol and hashish. Ana laid down a wreath of Gerbera daisies, crossed herself, and rested her chin on her chest. He merely stared at the tips of his shoes, rocking forward and back. He passed the time by drawing in the gravel with the tip of his umbrella. He glanced around at the names on the other stones, evaluating the neighborhood around his daughter's grave. She was the youngest in that part of the cemetery, there could be no doubt about it, apart from the rockers who drank beer and then urinated all over the walls. When Ana finished praying, he took her by the arm, and they headed for the exit. A slightly putrid smell of roses floated in the air, so he grabbed her elbow and quickened his pace. A magpie cawed at them from the railings at the entrance; it was a bird like any other, a black and white corvus with green-blue iridescence on its tail. He waved his arm to frighten it away, but the magpie redoubled its caws. His wife looked at him, as if seeking an explanation for the bird's behavior. He shrugged his shoulders and waved his arms again, forcefully this time, as if wanting to disperse a herd of cows that had stopped on the highway, but far from being scared off, the bird rose to its full height on the railings. He thought that if he'd had a shotgun, he would have killed it right then and there. He considered hurling a stone at it. "What's the matter with that bird?" asked Ana.

A dog prowling around the entrance to the cemetery barked at the magpie. It was an old German shepherd, barely capable of moving its hindquarters, its eyes masked by cataracts. It barked furiously, hoarsely. He didn't know which to frighten away, the dog or the bird, but his gesticulations only succeeded in exciting them both. His wife pleaded with him for them to leave. Behind the dog, a man appeared, a tiny beret pulled over his head. He swung a broom in the air, at hip height. By this time, three more magpies had joined the chorus from the top of a cypress. There was a sense of gregarious ferocity in their calls. Ana yanked at the sleeve of his raincoat. "Let's get out of here," she said, but he bent down to pick up a stone, though he wasn't sure who to throw it at, the dog barking more and more loudly, the groundskeeper, or one of the birds. The guard had managed to grab the dog by the tail and gestured to them to get out of there, but the German shepherd turned around with surprising agility and made as if to bite, without seeing who it was attacking, with the instinctive perceptiveness of the blind, opening its mouth full of chipped teeth, yellowed as if by nicotine. It latched onto the guard's hand. In an ingenious, effective move, his wife grabbed the umbrella from him and, opening and closing it energetically, advanced, *flop, flop, flop,* toward the dog, which meekly retreated into its kennel. The guard clenched his lips in pain. The bite had sliced through a nail and the skin of his phalange hung loose, pink and translucent. Alarmed by the cawing of the birds, they sought refuge in the car. Ana dressed the wound with a handkerchief. On the way to the hospital, the groundskeeper couldn't explain why his dog, Tula, had bitten him; they'd been together for fourteen years, it had never bitten anybody, not even the troublemakers that hung around the cemetery at night. Until then, it had simply barked. It was a very obedient animal. He suggested putting it down, it might have lost its mind, this happened to animals that were very old, he said. The man accepted the money Ana offered as compensation, and they left him at the entrance to the nearest hospital. On the way home, they discussed the details of the incident, Ana's intrepid gesture with the umbrella, his own inability to frighten those birds out of a Hitchcock movie. They seemed relieved it was all over. He noticed how the racket of birds and dogs had banished any reference to Laura. He smiled on thinking it had just been a joke, but he didn't share this thought with Ana. It must have been a code of signals one had only to know how to interpret, clues as subtle as the twitching of a net curtain, a whisper behind a partition wall, a tickling on the back of the neck, signs that, as with plagues, start revealing themselves little by little, in the insistent flight of a fly, or the presence of insects in the bathtub, insignificant signs, the revelation of which presages the arrival of something one can only surrender to without putting up any resistance. That's what it must have been. A joke of his dead daughter's. But he didn't explain his theory, he just said he would have to find a good cleaner to get rid of the blood stains on the car's upholstery.

He surprises himself with a second cigarette between his fingers. He flaps his hand, as if driving flies away from his face. He gets up from the tree trunk with sudden urgency. He crushes the cigarette butt against the crust of lichen covering the bark. He hears a crack behind him. He grasps his cane. Bends down to put himself at the height of the shadow moving behind the bushes. It could be the stray dog that sometimes prowls around the house in search of scraps of food. He picks up a stone. The shape emerges from the undergrowth. He has never seen a fox so close before. They look at each other, united by a bond of atavistic mistrust. The fox pants with its jaws wide open, watches him, prepared to accept whatever might happen now that this man is also staring at it, standing there, ready to pounce, armed with a cane and a stone. It sees this figure, but does not sense the predatory instinct of the men shouting on the other side of the highway or the ferocity of their hunting dogs, whose barks can no longer be made out. It hesitates for a moment between retracing its steps or slipping slowly past, toward the promise of freedom coming from the mountain, on the other side of the tree line. The man drops the stone. The fox walks unhurriedly past, watching him the whole time, and the air carries a scent it has never smelled before, except on some of the animals left in the ravine by shepherds, animals whose remains it sometimes feeds on, an impression that is mixed with other, stronger smells, but it finds nothing threatening in them, so it keeps moving away from the figure of the man, leaving it behind, and forgetting it as soon as it reaches the bend in the river.

The sound of the siren pierces the forest. He lifts his binoculars. On the shoulder of the highway is a fire engine, and several men running toward the scene of the accident; he identifies the figure of Jeremías approaching the car with a beach ball under his arm. He sees him stop next to one of the doors and crouch down without letting go of the ball. He lies down on the ground and gesticulates as if talking to somebody inside the car. He gets up and takes a few indecisive steps, not knowing what direction to go in. Suddenly, he puts his hands on his head and the ball bounces at his feet. A man dressed in a reflective vest pushes him away from the scene of the accident. The two men walk now toward the gas station. Jeremías continues gesticulating, and his companion puts an arm around his shoulder. The red and blue lights of an ambulance flash next to the alfalfa field. Another man spreads out a thermal blanket next to the wreck of the car. On the other side of the highway, an iodine-colored dog runs up and down the shoulder. A hunter kicks at the bushes. He holds an unlit cigarette butt between his teeth. The others stare up at the sky with their shotguns on their shoulders, scanning, as if expecting the arrival of a low-flying flock of woodpigeons. But in that angle of clear sky, the only thing that can be seen is the peaceful flight of a black kite.

6

One would have to be a tireless mole coming from the forest to be able to reach the notebook that's waiting, buried in the garden, wrapped in a plastic bag, beneath the hydrangeas. At the beginning of its journey in search of the promised land, it had to go around a gas pipe running perpendicular to the house, the route of which indicated the direction its fledgling tunnel should take. It dug earth, left the forest behind, the familiar territory crisscrossed by thick oak roots, and bored through the darkness until it reached a no-man's-land so dry and packed with garbage it seemed to promise nothing good. The crossing through that desolate subsoil led it to the discovery of a cemetery for old farming implements and fragments of Celtiberian pottery, a few coins, but its instinct told it this wasteland was nothing more than the test every adventure requires, since this was the place where others had perished before him, fumigated by insecticides, suffocated between successive layers of gravel and archaeological remains, or detected in the open by the cat watching from the lounge chair in the garden. And although the geological strata bore witness to endless disappearances, defeats, and wars, the adventurous mole did not fall into despair but carried on slowly, blindly and silently, leaving behind other fragments—this time some Roman jewelry, two Carlist bayonets, and a shell from the Civil War—until it reached the garden fence. It got past the final obstacle at the border by digging on a night with no moon, which protected it from the cat's watchful gaze. In the early morning, the nutritious smell of humus indicated its efforts were about to be rewarded. The tunnel came out in the promised garden. In a state of excitement, it sniffed the fragrance of a paradise of black earth and wet grass, the olfactory signs of a habitat in which a commune of worms and slugs, carefree and peaceful, had proliferated freely, oblivious to the dangers that might come from outside, from the other side of the fence, their only occupation being to enjoy, generation after generation, the surpluses of an Eden from which rivers of organic nutrients and mineral salts would never cease to flow.

Blinded by hunger and predatory euphoria, the mole received its first reward. It devoured a translucent worm, thick as a pinkie finger. A few languid shakes were the entirety of that decadent invertebrate's resistance. It supplemented this first banquet with half a dozen white larvae and a flaccid, medium-sized slug that it swallowed down unhurriedly, savoring its watery, slightly salty texture with just a hint of minerals and fertile clay. It was dozing next to the roots of some hydrangeas when it noticed a very different smell, of cellulose and plastic, coming from a shape buried next to the roots, arousing its exploratory instinct and an appetite that, worked up over a lifetime of penury and barbarity in the forest, had turned into gluttony.

One would have to be a mole to detect the hint of a teenager's perfume still clinging to the sheets of paper and to start sniffing in search of a nursery of maggots nesting between the pages, or perhaps a colony of tiny crustaceans—a mole intent on the idea of rounding off its own private banquet with a dessert of tender little snails, throwing precaution to the wind, rummaging around in the paper of the notebook and suddenly feeling the need to come up to the surface because beneath the weight of the bag, the tunnel has given way, with a landslide that has blocked the passage of air. It digs in the direction of the surface in search of oxygen, but fate has decreed that it will emerge in the very place where, having observed some suspicious movements of earth from the porch, the cat is now waiting, and the mole doesn't even have time to feel the early morning air, since the cat, trapping it between its claws, with little effort, almost disdainfully, sinks its canines into the mole, breaking its back. A slight crack between the jaws, and it's all over. Polanski waves the dead mole around in an unnecessary display of skill, oblivious to the man shaking a box of Whiskas on the porch.

"Another mole, Polanski?" he asks, blowing out a bubble of steam.

The cat looks at him without letting go of its prey. The roots of the hydrangeas peep out from the disturbed earth. The man feels the cold of morning and tightens the belt on his bathrobe. He checks the dampness of the frost with the toe of his slipper and as if crossing over stones in a stream, in little jumps, approaches the scene of the hunt.

"What a mess," he says. He attempts to bury the tips of the roots showing through the earth. He straightens the battered stem of the plant. In vain, he tries to fix it back in the earth. He pats the ground flat, but the plant, exhausted, doubles over again. "Fucking Polanski," he mutters, and pulls the hydrangea out in one go, extracting a plastic bag that appears to be stuck to the roots like a spider nest. He gazes at the object in surprise, as if he had just caught a fish, especially since there is an incongruous sheet of paper poking out through the airtight seal.

Leaning over the kitchen table, he removes an oilskin notebook from the bag. Some of the pages crumble in his fingers. The majority form a sheaf of paper plastered together with organic matter. He manages to rescue a dozen sheets from the mass of cellulose paste and spreads them out on the table. He cleans the surfaces with the edge of a knife until the letters start to be visible. He remembers having seen a hair dryer, so he goes up to the second floor and searches in the bathroom cabinet. When he comes down, he is holding a red hair dryer that looks like a galactic weapon. He dries the pages and chooses those that still appear legible. The lines of writing cover the graph paper of the notebook with a healthy use of the margin, though the angled writing, with large dots like balloons on the *i*'s, descends to the right a little, falling off the dividing line. The line spacing is generous. The text appears to have been written in a hurry. He senses that the letters transmit cold and that, as he goes over them, this cold sticks to his fingertips as if they were frost.

Each entry is headed with a day of the week. His fingers tremble a little on the paper, and in a mechanical gesture he isn't entirely aware of, they drift until they locate a pack of cigarettes. He thinks the narrative recourse of a *found manuscript* is a joke in bad taste, a recourse that is clearly excessive, pushes him into a corner, places him under an obligation, but one he cannot ignore, since it is right there, on the kitchen table, like a forensic scientist's evidence in the light of a lamp.

He smokes with an anxiety he seemed to have already forgotten, and half a cigarette turns into a compact ember under his nose. He spreads the sheets on the floor, like a folding map, and tries to discover a chronological order, a meaning, possibly mistaken, he thinks, to this text, since there is nothing that immediately indicates the order in which they were written. He looks at the clock and orders a pizza over the phone. A girl's voice answers.

"Telepizza, how can I help you?"

"I'd like a four seasons pizza . . . and a Coke," he adds.

"Small, medium, or family-sized?"

"Normal," he replies, "a normal Coke."

"The pizza, sir—small, medium, or family-sized?" the clerk insists.

"Family-sized," he replies, feeling stunned.

"Thirty minutes," answers the voice, after noting down his order.

Three hours later, the cat has managed to prize open the now-cold box and detach an anchovy covered in oregano from the mozzarella. But the man doesn't seem to care, or hasn't even noticed the act of larceny, absorbed as he is, crouching on the floor, the pages from the notebook between his legs, failing to notice he has just run out of cigarettes with which to get through the night.

Tuesday the 11th.

I've never written about myself. I don't know why I've decided to do it now. Maybe if I do, I'll understand myself better—like seeing myself from the other side of the mirror. And seeing everybody else. It makes me blush just to think that somebody might read this, so when I've finished, I'll hide it somewhere nobody will ever find it, except me. I'd like to see myself without makeup, without deodorant or lipstick. I might even start to like myself.

Thursday the 26th.

I got off the bus for no particular reason; it wasn't laziness, it's just that the park looked nice, just like the light, the air, and everything. To hell with my classes. I sat on the first bench I came across, facing the lake. There was a mime artist and people jogging in tracksuits. The water reflected everything. An old man came and sat down next to me. He smelled of cognac. I hate the smell of cognac. I hate the smell of cigar smoke. I hate the smell of sweat. The heels on his shoes were very worn down. His ankles, which were soft and fat, stuck out. He asked for a cigarette, I said no. His eyes were very red. I don't smoke, I said, and he grunted. He marched off, saying all women were whores. I also left, in the opposite direction, toward the mime artist. I had time to kill, so I bought myself a cookie and shared it with the fish in the pond, but when I got home, Mom asked me about my classes.

She seemed to have guessed. She's like that. It's enough for me to do something wrong, and she senses it. She sometimes dreams things that later happen. She sleepwalked as a child and used to open closets and pack a suitcase. Or so she says. The point is she asked me, "So how were your classes?" I didn't know what to say, maybe the school had called to ask why I was absent. I think I was a little obvious about it. She got a bit annoyed, but not too much. I always get good grades at the end of the year. She reminded me I'm going to college next year and have to make more of an effort. Dad didn't say a word, though. He lives enclosed in his bubble of air, just like the fish in the pond.

Friday the 7th.

I have a collection of postcards: New York, Shanghai, Prague, Lima, Rabat, South Africa, Tokyo, Moscow, Naples. I have a cat. I have almost blond hair. I have two girl friends. I have a photo album. I have a sense of fear.

Wednesday the 14th.

I liked going for walks with my grandpa. I miss the way he used to look at me, over the top of his glasses. Like the day we came across Polanski mewing in the rubble. We had left earlier than usual, which annoyed my mother because she thought Grandpa was turning me into a tomboy with all those walks in the hills and all those bugs. We were walking alongside the ravine when we heard a meow. Grandpa leaned over and pointed into the bottom. There was a ball of fur, on top of a tractor part. There were thistles and glistening pieces of glass and the rusty part the kitten was mewing on top of. "It's looking for its mother, who won't be long," Grandpa said, pushing me gently so we could continue with our walk. But I knew he'd said this because he didn't want to worry me. Besides, Grandpa was in the habit of not intervening. He said the hand of man wasn't good for animals that lived in the countryside. "Touch a wild animal, and it will never be the same again," he used to say. I couldn't stop looking at the little cat. I tugged at his shirtsleeve. "It's lost," I said. It mewed in our direction. Its eyes were green. It walked back and forth across the rusty iron, checking the edges. I tugged at his sleeve again. "Help him," I said, and Grandpa looked at me over the top of his glasses. "Help him, please." He sighed. Tested the ground with his cane and went down into the rubble. "Your mother is going to kill me," he said, and the cat mewed even louder. Grandpa picked him up by the scruff of his neck, and the cat stopped mewing, closed its eyes, and became very quiet, hanging in the air. It took him a while to bring him up, the broken glass crunched under his boots. I stretched out my arms and he gave him to me. He purred while digging his claws into my shoulder. I remember Grandpa's labored breathing and his slightly bleary eyes. When we got home, my dad gave it the name Polanski. My mom nearly had a fit.

Now, while I'm writing, Polanski is sitting next to me. He's looking at me like he knew I was the one who rescued him from the ravine. Maybe Grandpa is somewhere around here, too, watching me without talking. Right at this very moment.

Friday the 23rd.

Yesterday I helped my mom tidy out the storage room. Lots of things turned up: stories, my first school notebook, and a drawing of the three of us, on the beach. Dad is under a beach umbrella, reading a book, Mom is holding a starfish. I'm in the foreground, with freckles and pigtails. I didn't remember that drawing. I must have been nine or ten when I did it. I remember

Mom's swimsuit, which was blue and white, and the fact that I got my period for the first time that summer. I was a little frightened. I couldn't go swimming. My mother bought me a box of crayons and some paper, so I did this drawing. I don't know how I would draw us now, perhaps at home, like feverish little animals, each in his lair—Dad bent over his desk, Mom sunbathing in the garden, me driving a car.

Monday the 1ˢᵗ.

I watch Dad lift his head from his books, the way he enters and leaves the house, so serious. A mute man. If everybody knew how weak he is, maybe they wouldn't respect him so much. The same thing happens when painters and artists come to our house and my mother serves canapés and glasses of iced champagne. They seem happy, but then each one goes back to his own private silence. They don't realize there are knots and splinters on their faces. They sleep in separate beds. My girl friends' parents don't sleep in separate beds. At least, not as far as I know. This house is like a hospital.

Sunday the 7ᵗʰ.

Yesterday was Mom's birthday. There is nothing more depressing than a family meal. I considered telling them I didn't feel well, but my dad guessed my intentions. I asked him what we were going to give her this time. "It's a surprise, from us both." I hate Sundays—sitting at the table after the meal, the cigarette smoke and my mother's forced laughter. How can they live like this? All adults are bored, you can tell by the way they walk, like they're carrying an invisible weight, by the way they talk and look at things. The world turns opaque before their eyes, and then their faces fall. My father's face fell some time ago.

133

That will never happen to me, I will never become like that, I don't want to be bored, or sad. I imagined us all sitting at a table in a restaurant, our faces falling on top of our plates.

We went out to eat at a cider bar on the other side of the valley. There was a playground and a garden and a reservoir with boats, and the sun made my arms itch. Uncle Óscar turned up on his motorcycle. His latest girlfriend was sitting behind him—a girl with a perky butt and a fish face. I like Uncle Óscar a lot, so slim, with his boots and fighter pilot sunglasses. One day, Uncle Óscar came to pick me up at school on his bike. Everybody in the class's jaws dropped open when they saw me put on my helmet and race away. The noise of the engine reverberated down the street and I clung to his waist. I could see the asphalt flying past, and his gloved hands, and his strong arms covered in blond hair. One day I'd like to have a boyfriend like him.

I didn't say a word the whole meal. What would I talk about? My mother staring at Uncle Óscar's girlfriend out of the corner of her eye, my father staring at her, as well, and Uncle Óscar telling jokes and asking me, "Lo, what's up with Lo? Sighs come out of her strawberry mouth." He's the only one I allow to say such things.

My father went to the car and came back with the present under his arm. There was no need to ask what it was—a painting. Uncle Óscar started singing Happy Birthday. His girlfriend moved her silicone-swollen lips. My mother tore open the wrapping paper—St Mark's Square in winter. "It's by a very promising local painter. He has presence and a sure touch, see," said my father, pointing at the cathedral and horses. She blew him a kiss off the palm of her hand. Then Uncle Óscar got out a camera. He said he'd bought it on his latest trip to New York. The camera shone in his hands when he lifted it toward us. He

134

told us to move closer together, he was going to use it for the first time to take a family portrait of us. "Look at me, Lo," he said. The sun was behind him, and the leaves on the trees were reflected in the water, which looked like a sheet of gold.

Monday the 21ˢᵗ.
Had my period all day. From my bed to the sofa, from the sofa to my bed. Pale face, legs as heavy as two logs.

Tuesday the 12ˢᵗ.
I knew they wouldn't like Antonio. He's six years older than me, he smokes, drinks, has a ponytail, and drives an old, beat-up car. When we went into Samby, Sandra told us to look at the boy in the black T-shirt. Claudia said he was an old man, but I liked him, so slim, with his pirate ponytail and deep black eyes. I stared at him, and he stared back. He came over, and we started talking. He cracked a joke about my eyes, said they were very pretty, looked like two minerals. Then he opened his wide. He made me laugh. My friends were burning with envy, especially Sandra, who was the one who'd spotted him first. Sandra isn't ugly, but if I were a man, her pimples would give me the shivers. Claudia watched us from the other side of the bar while sipping a piña colada. We talked about movies. He also liked horror movies. He knew a lot about movies, and about music as well. He studied computer engineering. He told me all about computer viruses and the effects they can have on a computer, and I could see out of the corner of my eye that my friends were growing impatient. After a while, Sandra came over and asked me what I wanted to do, since they were going home. Antonio said he had a car and could take me. I shrugged my shoulders. I smiled at Sandra, but she twisted her mouth and left. It got late. As we

were leaving the city, I watched the orange streetlights and the wet asphalt going past on the other side of the car window. He asked me if I would like to go to the movies, we arranged to meet the following weekend. When he started calling me at home, I rushed to grab the phone before my parents. Mom was dying of curiosity, so she did her best to be near the phone. I remember the expression she got when she put her ear to the receiver and heard a man's voice asking for me. She raised her eyebrows and handed me the phone as if it had turned into a snake. Then came the questions and the conversation with cups of green tea on the porch table, just like the day she explained to me where children come from. Since then, we hadn't spoken about sex. The poor woman got all flustered, and I didn't know what to do with myself, either, when she told me we had to take precautions because she didn't want to see my life ruined by a slip-up. That's the word she used—a slip-up. And she added, "If you want, we can go and see the gynecologist . . ." She reminded me I was still under age. "Mom, please . . . ," I begged her. I thought that was the typical kind of legalistic argument my father would use. She would never have come up with something like that. I reminded her it was only a few months until I turned eighteen. Her face hid behind the steam coming from the teapot as she hurriedly discussed condoms and pills. Poor Mom. I wonder how they do it. I can't imagine my father putting a condom there. I don't think they do it very much. In fact, I don't think they do it at all. My father steered clear of the subject of Antonio from the very beginning. He played dumb, didn't want to know who this guy calling his daughter was, but I felt he was watching me, especially when I left home with eye makeup on while outside Antonio kept honking the horn.

136

Wednesday the 13th.

My parents met Antonio on the day of Grandpa's funeral. They were too sad to think about their daughter's boyfriend. And I was too sad to think about the impression Antonio would make on them, with his ponytail and black T-shirt. There were my father and Uncle Óscar, in black ties, and my mother with her chin on her chest. After the funeral, there were people I'd never set eyes on in my life, kissing me on the cheek and saying how pretty you are, Laura, really, how pretty. Then it all became very distant, especially when we went outside and I saw Antonio's head poking out from the crowd. I hugged him. Felt his cold, sweaty skin. I hadn't cried all day. When my father told me Grandpa had died, I couldn't shed a single tear, I could only imagine him in bed, asleep, but dead—dead, but asleep—his heart having stopped, without making a noise, like an old clock, under his pajamas. And that image was the only thing I could feel. I only started crying when I felt my head resting on Antonio's shoulder. That was when the floodgates opened, in front of everybody. He took me by the arm and shook my father's hand very seriously and said, "I'm sorry," and my father replied, "Thank you." And that was it.

Monday the 30th.

I hate math, I hate matrices, the number e, equations. When I'm not interested in something, I'm incapable of giving it my attention; numbers evaporate, signs, unknown quantities that have to be cleared. So I've flunked math again. Unless I'm careful, I'll flunk it again in June, and that would be a disaster, just the excuse my parents need to redirect their daughter's path far away from Antonio, they'll send me off to a summer school abroad. To Ireland. I'm not logical, and sometimes that makes Antonio nervous, though what he does isn't all that logical, either. Otherwise, why spend so much money on cocaine? My father surrounds himself with books, looks after his hydrangeas, my mother listens to opera and drinks green tea. What's logical about all of that? When we're in the car, I say to him, "Look, Antonio, what a beautiful sunset," and he smiles without looking away from the road and then strokes my cheek. To begin with, I was ashamed for him to see my breasts, they're so small. I shouldn't have swum as a child, but my mother insisted on taking me to swimming lessons and off I went each day to swim, so now I look like a boy from behind. But Antonio says I have a very nice body, and he strokes my shoulders and kisses me on the neck. Then I don't have any doubts, and everything strikes me as clean and perfect, pure, the way numbers are supposed to be.

Wednesday the 11th.

The cleaning lady couldn't come today, so it's up to me to tidy the kitchen. My father has just finished eating as I collect the plates. I can see his head, so similar to Grandpa's, his short hair, a little gray. He's wearing that loud tie my mother gave him. He doesn't like it, but he wears it all the same. I take the plate from under his nose while he polishes off his glass of wine. I wait for him to finish, standing behind him. He leaves the glass on the table, a little white wine still in the bottom. I look at him and for a moment feel like giving him a kiss on the head, like he was a child, and telling him, "Dad, I love you very much," but instead of that, I take his empty glass and he leaves the kitchen, his tie like a yellow stain in the middle of his weary figure.

Sunday the 16th.

I'm not what others think I am. Only I know the truth. My parents think I'm spoiled, Antonio thinks I'm good, my teachers say I'm very intelligent, but only I know I'm selfish and bad and sometimes have terrible thoughts. I don't know why I have these thoughts, but I do. Sometimes I would like nothing to exist—those trees, the air—and for my parents not to have brought me into the world. On days like today, I think this and I know it won't pass and that these thoughts will come back another day, and another, from time to time, like the clouds coming over from the other side of the valley. I've spent the afternoon looking at photo albums. My mother so pretty, with a miniskirt and a white purse, my father wearing a tuxedo, on the deck of a cruise ship. They're happy. At least, they look it. They remind me of the characters in those boring, black-and-white movies who drink champagne and a piano plays and then they kiss on the deck of the ship, or they drink tea in a garden with hedges, under a white parasol, because it's always sunny, like on a Sunday that never ends. At the bottom of the photograph is written, "Cyprus, 1972." The island is visible in the background. Then there's me, in another photo—a round head peeping out from a long gown, and my mother, looking pale, holding me on her lap. My father's head appears in one corner, he's standing next to us. He smiles shyly, but looks proud. His face hadn't fallen back then, it didn't even look like that could ever happen to him, with that sharp profile and those dark black bangs, and in the center of his forehead there was a shine, a ring of gold that's gone now, and doesn't shine. On the back, my mother has written in her pointed handwriting, "June 11*th*, 1981." My birthday.

Friday the 31*st*.

Antonio has gone to Amsterdam with some friends. Now that I think about it, I still haven't met his friends. He introduced me once to a man with a pockmarked face and very thin lips. He was the owner of a club. He told us to drink whatever we liked, his treat, he was very attentive, but I didn't like the way he smiled at me. Antonio told him to wait for him. Then the two of them went off and left me alone. They sat at a table in the back of the club and talked for ages. That's Antonio's only friend. He said he'd call me as soon as he got to Amsterdam. I didn't even consider the possibility of going with him, nor did he suggest it. I haven't seen my girl friends for a while, but I don't feel like calling them. They'll have gone to the movies. I took my poster of Tom Cruise off my bedroom wall some time ago, but I'll bet they're still discussing who's better looking, Mel Gibson or Brad Pitt. Then they'll have gone to drink apple liqueur in the bar district. I miss Antonio. I hope he calls me.

Wednesday the 10th.
   Yesterday Polanski caught a blackbird. The porch was covered in black feathers, and drops of blood glistened on the tiles. It was a very pretty bird—an orange beak, the color of a peach. I said to him, "Polanski, you're a bad cat," and he just looked at me from the deckchair like he didn't know me.

Sunday the 8th.
   I talked to Antonio and I think that was the best part of the day. He sounded very happy. I was waiting for him to tell me he missed me, but he didn't. Uncle Óscar came for lunch. He whistled when he saw me. "Shame you're my niece, otherwise I'd make a pass at you, Lo," he said. "Me too," I said and had a fit of the giggles. My mother gave him a reproving look. I like it when he says these things. I think he's the only member of this family who could understand me. Mother had cooked a dish of green-colored roe. Uncle Óscar made a very funny remark

140

about the food, and I had another fit of the giggles. He then explained that he was going to Thailand to do a photo-essay for an American magazine. My father didn't open his lips the whole meal. Last night he had a fight with my mother. It was worse than other times. I pressed my ear against the wall, but could barely make out what they were saying. I could hear his hoarse voice and mother crying on the other side of the wall. I got a little bit frightened because I heard the sound of a glass object hitting the floor and my father's hoarse voice again. Then nothing. And yet the sound seemed to float over us during the meal— my father slicing into the roe in silence, my mother laughing halfheartedly at Uncle Óscar's jokes, me at one end of the table, Grandpa's empty chair at the other. Over dessert, Uncle Óscar said he'd broken up with his girlfriend. "How many is that now?" my mother asked. My father answered for him, "He's lost count." Deep down, he's jealous of him. Uncle Óscar comes and goes as he pleases, rides a 1000 cc motorcycle, and has lots of girlfriends. He's capable of discussing any subject and can tell very amusing stories about some of the people he's met: drug traffickers, mercenaries, gangsters . . . My father, on the other hand, writes art reviews, gives classes, has a house he bought thanks to his wife's inheritance, and a daughter who's started wearing too much makeup.

Thursday the 11ᵗʰ.

My birthday. I was expecting something different; after all, one doesn't turn eighteen every day. I thought it would be something special, but it wasn't at all. Antonio gave me an old, silver lighter he brought back from Holland. He insisted I try some coke to celebrate, but I said no. We saw each other for barely half an hour in VIPS, he had to study for a computer exam. He

141

was very nervous. He's grown thinner. While talking, he kept an eye on the entrance to the restaurant. He looked like a frightened animal. A blond man had been following him all day, a Russian with almond-shaped eyes. I asked him who it was and why they were looking for him, but he said it was better I didn't know. He kept on looking over his shoulder at the street. On the other side of the window, there was only a blind woman selling lottery tickets. Nobody else. He didn't fix his eyes on me, they seemed to run all over the table. After he'd left, I felt a heaviness in the pit of my stomach.

My mother gave me a competition swimsuit; Sandra and Claudia, a tattoo. That was the best. We went to a tattoo parlor, and I chose a red drawing of a dragon. I thought Antonio would like it. Sandra wanted me to have it put on my shoulder, but I said I would look like a sailor. Claudia said the best place was on my ankle. I had it put on my back, under the nape of my neck, that way, with my hair down, it can't be seen. I suppose today was important, but I don't feel anything special.

Monday the 9*th*.

I sometimes remember things. Today, for example, I recall my first memory. Why does one remember such things on certain days? I wonder if there's something that triggers such memories. I don't know. What I do know is that in this memory, I'm throwing stones into the river next to my father. I can see him, dressed in a jacket and tie, standing on an orange digger. I don't know what such a large, flame-colored machine is doing in my memory, but the fact is it's there, and my father is standing on it, looking very elegant, like he was about to go off to a wedding banquet. I'm on the riverbank. I don't know what river it is, but there are green rushes, and dragonflies flitting over the surface, and pebbles on the bank. *My father jumps off the orange-colored machine and comes toward me, I can see his large hand coming closer and stroking my face, he bends down, picks up a very flat stone, and throws it at the water. The stone skips across the surface. He encourages me to do the same, and I do. There we are. I don't know for how long, perhaps a few minutes, hours, or days, because time is lost in the memory, like the light reflected on the dragonflies' wings, and the drops of water exploding on the surface. It's a good memory, my best memory. One day, I asked him what we were doing there, why we went to that river, what he was doing standing on a digger. He looked at me, thoughtfully, and said he didn't know.*

Thursday the 21ˢᵗ.

I passed my driving test. On the first try. Claudia and Sandra came with me to my appointment for the driving portion. I'd like to have a motorcycle, but I know my parents don't even want to consider such a possibility. They had an argument last night.

Friday the 18ᵗʰ.

The fact is I'd only ever kissed a few boys, little else. Over summer vacation last year, I went a bit further. It was with an English boy, Peter, I met on the beach. We swam together for a while and then chatted by the seashore. On the last day of vacation, we went for a walk. We had a pizza and then went to a club. He drank loads of beer and I downed shots of apple liqueur. After a while, I felt pretty dizzy, but I danced much better, and Peter looked very handsome. We kissed on the dance floor. We went outside. I could feel a weight in my head, sweat on my neck, and Peter's hand grabbing my waist. We ended up *lying on the beach, next to the sea. I remember the black water and white foam. There were stars. I asked him if he could tell the difference between the stars and the planets, but he was much more interested in sticking his nose down my cleavage. We kissed lying down, he caressed me and started to undress me, his wet hands covered in sand and rubbing my breasts. He'd pulled down his pants, and his butt shone white in the moonlight. Suddenly I had the impression this wasn't what I wanted, his breath stank of beer and cigarettes, his face was contorted into an ugly expression. He panted on top of me, laboring away, like a chimpanzee. I felt something moving inside my stomach, like I was flying on a plane. I didn't want to see his butt, so white it resembled a cheese. That's what I felt. So I pushed him away. He looked at me uncomprehendingly. All I wanted was to get the sand off my body. I walked to the edge of the water and vomited. He said something in English I didn't understand, but by the time I'd recovered, he was already walking off, kicking the sand.*

I don't know if I want to make love to Antonio. He keeps saying we should, but I'm a little afraid. I talked to Claudia about it yesterday. She said if I really loved him, there shouldn't be any problem, but I think she just said that to calm me down.

Tuesday the 20th.

I would have liked to have had a brother or sister. I think about it sometimes. I would like there to have been other voices at home, someone to talk to, though brothers and sisters, it would seem, don't talk to each other all that much. They quarrel when they're kids and then meet up from time to time, like my father and Uncle Óscar. I know my parents tried to have kids for years, then I turned up, out of the blue. When I'm older, I'd like to have lots of kids and lots of cats. Claudia has two older brothers, and Sandra, a little brother. They envy me because I have a very large bedroom all to myself, but there are times, like today, when the house is silent, like it's holding its breath, and outside, the forest also seems to be waiting for something. There's a strange sense of anguish that merges with the smell of the green tea my mother prepares at all hours because she says it has antioxidant properties and prevents cancer. Perhaps I should talk to her. Tell her what I feel (but what do I feel?). I don't know what she feels, either. I wonder if she would be happy somewhere else, if instead of living here with a husband called Gabriel and a daughter called Laura, she lived somewhere else, on the coast, next to the sea, for example, and was married to another man, somebody nice and romantic, who looked after her and made her feel wanted. Unique. Does she ever think about it? Does Mom regret her life?

Thursday the 11th.

My parents have gone. My father had to attend a conference in Sweden. Then he planned to take a few days' vacation. As a girl, my mother traveled to lots of countries. Her father was a diplomat, her mother's family owned a shipbuilding company. She says she was very happy. My father, however, hates traveling, change. He needs routine, like the fish in the pond. My mother doesn't talk much about her parents, though I think she misses them. She never stopped wanting to travel, even after her parents died in a plane crash in Tenerife. I don't remember them at all.

Friday the 12th.

It's wonderful being home alone. I got up early, fed Polanski, and then went to school. When I got back, I ate whatever I felt like, which is to say, not very much (I think I'm getting a bit fat).

I studied math and then went to swim at the pool—the water underneath me, like a liquid whale, the water's volume and my own body on top of that transparent, blue mass. In the evening, my parents called. They were in Stockholm. They'd had smoked herring for dinner. They sounded happy. Tomorrow, Antonio's coming to spend the day at the house. Butterflies in my stomach.

Sunday the 14th.

   I am no longer a virgin. The whole day passed very slowly, like each minute was leading up to this event. I noticed it as soon as Antonio arrived. There was a kind of invisible tension between us. Polanski arched his back and hissed at him. I'm glad the cat can't talk, because I promised my parents I wouldn't bring Antonio here. He liked the house a lot, he looked at the paintings and furniture and whistled in admiration. Then I took him for a walk around the local area. We took the path through the forest. We bought cigarettes at the gas station. Jeremías stared at Antonio distrustfully, like he was a delinquent. I almost burst out laughing. "Everybody here seems to want to protect you from me," he said. We crossed the Roman bridge, and I showed him my favorite spot. The poplars are yellow now, next to the stream. It's so pleasant there, it's difficult to find a better place, but I don't think Antonio knew how to appreciate it. What's more, he scratched his cheek on a branch. He's clearly never set foot in the countryside before. Grandpa would have laughed at him a lot. We gathered chestnuts and in the evening roasted them in the fire. Then we watched a horror movie. I squeezed his hand a lot, and he laughed when he saw how I covered my face every time the murderer jumped out with a chainsaw. Polanski gazed at me from the floor with wide-open eyes, like he could sense something was about to happen. At the end of the movie, Antonio started *kissing me on the sofa. I felt this is what I had been waiting for, this and what followed, whatever it might be. I just let myself go, without fear. We went up to my bedroom, taking off our clothes on the stairs. I removed the teddy bears from my bed, and then his body was on top of mine, and his saliva, and his soft skin. It hurt, but less than I had imagined. I felt him shuddering inside me, and then a warmth in my belly. I clenched my teeth. His body shook like a reed. Then he fell to one side. I felt like something was biting me between my legs, then nothing, and a tiny little wave of heat. "Is that it?" I thought. Antonio kept his eyes closed for a while, facing the wall, then lit a cigarette. He was naked, and his breastbone stood out on his chest. I asked him if he loved me. He said of course he did. Why else would he be there? Now that I think about it, I was rather disappointed. It wasn't what I expected, or like in those movies when two people moan and seem to be having a great time and to love each other a lot. But it was nice to doze off together and to feel that I had changed and was different. It was an important day. Tomorrow I'll have to tell Claudia all about it.*

Monday the 15th.

Smoking. Thinking about Antonio. How good it is to be home alone.

Tuesday the 16th.

My parents got back this afternoon. They didn't look well. When they behave like this, I think I hate them. Perhaps if I did something serious, they would wake up—I don't know, set fire to the living room, for example, or my father's library, or behead the hydrangeas . . . I'm sure they'd send me to see a shrink.

Saturday the 27th.

    Polanski catches a moth that was sleeping on the curtains. He tortures it slowly on the floor. The moth tries to escape, shakes its one wing, but only manages to turn around in circles. He looks at it without much interest, his pupils dilate a bit. He jumps on top of it, then chews it and shakes his head until the moth disappears between his sharp teeth. My mother went to spend the afternoon in town. Dad asked if I wanted to go with him to the gas station to buy the newspaper, like when I was a child and Jeremías would give me sweets. I said no, I had to study for my next math exam. Mom was late coming back from town. She was wearing her blue dress. It looks really good on her, and she only wears it on special occasions, like when she had to pose for the portrait in the living room. She wears that dress because she thinks it makes her look young and pretty. Perhaps I should talk to her. Or to them both. But what would I say?

Sunday the 28th.

    Haven't heard from Antonio.

Monday the 1st.

    I tried calling Antonio several times, but only got his answering machine. I spent the day walking around the city. I didn't feel like seeing anybody. I sometimes have the impression that the three of us—Mom, Dad, and I—do everything we can to not see each other, to not have to talk. The three of us are running away. That's my impression, at least—a structure that is slowly dissolving. And nobody does anything to stop it. The city had withdrawn into itself, like me, under a sky that seemed to have been made out of dirty plaster. Despite the fact that spring has arrived, it snowed in the mountains. Everybody's talking about it. With the cold, people have turned in on themselves and are oblivious to everything. Having wandered through the arcade in the plaza, I went into a bar to have some coffee. The owner was arguing with his wife about an order that hadn't arrived. I took some photos of myself in a photo booth. When I saw them, I said to myself I was changing a lot. I didn't look too bad, all things considered. I think I've lost a bit of weight. I'll give one to Antonio. On the way home, I thought I saw my father. At least, the car was the same as his, an off-white BMW. He was stopped at a traffic light, but somehow didn't look like himself. I banged on the glass of the bus window. He didn't see me. How strange it is to watch somebody outside of their normal context, while they're working, or walking down the street on their own, or out shopping. Seen like this, he looked like an interesting man, his hands resting on the steering wheel, with his sharp profile and straight nose. His eyes were squinted in concentration, like he was listening to the news on the radio. A normal guy, in a normal city, for whom, no doubt, things weren't going too badly.

Thursday the 12th.

It's like he's evaporated. Claudia says I should forget about him. I have a knot in my throat. Over lunch, I told my father I'd seen him in his car. "That wasn't me," he said, "I have a class then, where else would I be?" My mother looked at him over the rim of her glass. Then she asked me, "You also have a class at that time, what were you doing on a bus?" I suddenly felt the blood rushing to my face, and I stood up from the table. "You're a couple of idiots." That's what I said.

Wednesday the 26th.

Study, I have to focus on studying. Claudia insisted I should forget all about Antonio. It may be for the best, but I can't get

149

used to the idea of not having him by my side. Sandra just shrugged her shoulders, the dumb idiot. She's done something to her face, she has fewer pimples now. I miss Grandpa. I'd like him to be near, right here, next to Polanski. Just going for a walk would help to clear my thoughts, just seeing him walk. Where is he, what's he thinking? I sometimes imagine he no longer has a face, or a body, or glasses, because he no longer needs them, and I suppose he's watching us, just like the light piercing the mist at the moment. Perhaps Polanski can see him and that's why he sometimes mews while staring up at the ceiling, like there was something there. Study, I have to study more. An hour each day, in the afternoon, after lunch. Then I can go and swim for a while. I'd like to dream of water.

Saturday the 7th.
   Haven't heard from Antonio.

Friday the 17th.
   Still keeping up my study and fitness program. The days are getting longer. Nothing to say, nothing to write. From home to school, from school to home, my lengthy shadow on the cobblestones in the street.

Tuesday the 30th.
   Yesterday I saw Antonio near the entrance to Samby. We almost crashed into each other. He was white as a sheet. He stuttered. Excused himself. He'd been traveling, then he'd been sick. He kept stumbling all over his words. He looked thinner, and uglier. He'd cut his hair off. You could see the skin on his skull. He said again that he'd been sick, something to do with his liver. "Is that all you have to say to me?" I asked, and

the stupid moron started crying. Then he confessed he'd gotten himself into a mess with drugs and owed a lot of money. He talked without looking me in the eye. He suggested I might be able to help him. I had a crumpled bill in my purse, so I gave it to him. Then I said I never wanted to see him again. Ever. When I got home, I threw away everything I had from him—a leather bracelet, a CD he'd lent me, the lighter he brought back from Amsterdam. I cried for the rest of the day.

Thursday the 4th.
  I'm just a silly girl.

Wednesday the 15th.
  Better off on my own, I tell myself. It's better like this. I went out with my girl friends again. We went to the movie theater and saw a vampire movie. It was a very nice love story. I even cried at the end. We stayed out at a club until two in the morning. I slept over at Sandra's house. The bed kept turning around me. I almost vomited.

Friday the 27th.
  I don't know if it's OK, and it frightens me a little to think about it. Even to write about it. But it's too late now—and who cares? After all, this is my diary. Nobody will know. I tell myself it doesn't matter, but if my parents found out, it would be a catastrophe. They haven't noticed anything. But if you think about it, how would they, when each of them is just gaping inside their own fishbowl? "These things happen, Lo, and I love you very much," said Uncle Óscar, though by now he wasn't Uncle Óscar anymore, but Óscar, just Óscar. Secrets are for keeping.

Wednesday the 10th.

Studying for my final exams. The light outside is inflamed with pollen. My mother has allergies, and I hear her sneezing on the next floor. I watch her come up the stairs with a hot chocolate, she ruffles my hair and sneezes again as she goes back down to the second floor. I like studying up here, in the attic, next to my father's library. I look at his university-professor glasses, his broad-tipped markers, and feel a strange sense of discomfort. Tubes of light are coming in through the window.

Friday the 31st.

Yesterday I went to the movie theater with Claudia to see a zombie movie. Absolute garbage. I couldn't help thinking about Óscar. On the way out, she said I looked very pretty. I couldn't explain why, not even to her, my best friend. She wouldn't understand.

Saturday the 15th

My grade on the final exams: 8.9. Everyone was very proud of me. It's decided—I'm going to study biology. To celebrate, we went out for dinner in a restaurant. Óscar stroked my knee under the table. My parents let me drink white wine during the dinner. We made toasts. After dinner, we stayed out on the porch. The two of us were alone. I kissed him. Nobody saw it, except for Polanski. The blood drained from Óscar's face. He almost died of fright.

Wednesday the 24th.

Summers before were long, never ending. Everything was like light reflected on the surface of the swimming pool—a sheet of

152

gold devoid of history or promises. Now time moves away, things come and go, and one can't do anything to stop it. Like sitting on a carousel. Even if I wanted to, would it be possible? Things move away from me—Polanski, evenings, my glass of milk, the blackbirds nesting next to the forest.

Saturday the 3rd

Óscar and I met up next to the stream. We spread a blanket out on the ground. The cicadas threshed the air. The air smelled of stalks of wheat. Our skin was a stalk of wheat. Lying there, naked, nobody could stop anything.

Monday the 17th.

They've bought me a car! Red, too, my favorite color. OK, to tell the truth, it's for the three of us, but I have their permission to use it. I gave them both a huge kiss. My mother's not very happy about it; it was Dad who insisted on giving it to me. I adore him. I'd love to run into that imbecile Antonio, so he could see me driving my car, with Óscar next to me and the music turned up really loud. I called Claudia and Sandra. The three of us will be able to make some amazing plans. Óscar gave it his approval and explained a whole bunch of things about the car to me. "Lo, you're a real woman now. You don't need anything else," he said while kicking a tire with the tip of his shoe. Mom stared at the car like it was a UFO. She kept on saying, "You will be careful, won't you, Laura?"

Wednesday the 13th.

I know what I'll do when I don't want to write in this diary anymore, I'll hide it somewhere nobody will ever find it, in the garden, underground. I am happy.

153

Thursday the 3rd.

I like listening to Óscar's stories. I've heard him tell some of them lots of times, but I don't mind. I think he always exaggerates a little, I'm not saying he lies, but I do think he exaggerates. I like his voice. It's not very deep, just a little metallic, but soft, almost soporific. It's the voice of an oboe. On the phone, I could mistake him for Dad. They're very similar in this way.

Tuesday the 20th.

I have a life, but now it seems to me I have two lives, or more: Laura out and about, Laura at home, Laura with Óscar. It's strange. Like living in different, parallel worlds. I enter one of them, then come out and jump over to another, like passing through walls of water. The strangest thing is that in spite of everything, it's still me; I see myself just the way I am. I know who I am, I know what I want. Why carry on writing?

Thursday the 18th.

Ever since college started, I've again had a strange feeling in the pit of my stomach. Óscar insists we should take care that nobody discovers us, but I love him, and he loves me, too. I wish I were ten years older so that I could go and live with him somewhere where it's always hot, the two of us together forever.

Saturday the 20th.

Next week, we'll go and spend Christmas up at the cabin. My ski clothes are ready, my boots and my parka. Óscar is coming on the weekend to have dinner with us. What else could I ask for?

Champagne commercials on TV. In the garden, the snow falls slowly, like in a dream.

He'd give his right hand for a cigarette. He searches in the closet, but only manages to salvage a few threads of tobacco from the pocket of his coat. He scours the drawers and then the liquor cabinet in the hope of finding a cigar, a dried-out, forgotten favor from some wedding, in a glass tube. Perhaps Jeremías could get him a pack of Ducados, or Bisontes, if that brand is still on the market, but he doesn't remember the number of the gas station. Where can the phone book be? He probably threw it on the last bonfire he had in the garden. Perhaps he could wrap up warm and walk to the gas station. He looks at his watch. It's absurd. It's two thirty in the morning. The rest of the night is a vacant lot. He imagines a black canvas. He abandons the pages of Laura's diary, resigned to the certainty of sleeplessness and anxiety. His depression does not pass unnoticed by the cat dozing in a ball on the kitchen counter. There are remains of anchovies scattered all over the floor; it's not difficult to deduce why the animal hasn't gone for its nocturnal outing.

He collapses on the sofa, and the sound of the TV muffles the laughter of the succubus, which he senses somewhere in the room, perhaps under the carpet, or in the hollow of the sculpture in the shape of an ostrich egg. He is grateful for the hypnosis of the news bulletin on an international channel. It takes him a while to realize he can't understand any of what the presenter is saying. She must be speaking Czech or something.

The screen is showing several images from a war. The greenish flares of tracer bullets replace the image of

Laura and her car concertinaed like a beer can. A group of soldiers creeps along a dune, their eyes illuminated in the darkness, like hares dazzled by a car's headlights, but the images are as unreal as the car on the alfalfa field seen through his binoculars, as unreal as Laura's own car, which he always imagined discarded on the hard shoulder of a mountain road, coated in frost. He stopped looking through the binoculars, in the conviction that the image of the bodies under the thermal blanket would illuminate Laura again, bring her back to life from out of the frozen iron, an inexpressive, blind, but desirous figure as alive as the voice that seems to rise from the pages of the diary now abandoned on the kitchen table.

He changes the channel, and the picture of a dark, young woman appears on the screen, a girl with a prominent bone structure and hair dyed platinum blond. Then a portrait, and a phone number. He deduces that the woman has gone missing. The TV presenter explains something in her incomprehensible language. He changes the channel, and the girl's face disappears, to be replaced by a car advertisement. On French Television 1, a weatherman predicts frosts across southern Europe. He focuses on the atmospheric symbols scattered all over the map. One symbol forecasts snow on either side of the Pyrenees. The resorts are working at full capacity, there are many miles of powder, perfect for skiing. He remembers the cottony sound of virgin snow, his leg sinking in up to the knee.

He huddles on the sofa without paying attention to Polanski's mewing, an abrupt, prolonged mewing, an alarming complaint that doesn't make sense at that hour of the morning. It's about to grow light, he thinks, or dreams, overcome by tiredness, relaxed by the lack of nicotine. Only the animal senses the movement of the anonymous observer toward the closet where Laura's red parka is hanging, the waterproof material still retaining the dewiness of snow and the artificial, slightly sickly smell of the car's almost brand-new upholstery. These smells evoke Laura's profile in the car window as she drives in the direction of the cabin near the ski resort where, like every year, they were going to celebrate Christmas Eve, and her hands clinging to the steering wheel, the skin on her knuckles turned white, tense and happy at the prospect of dinner, presents, Óscar's proximity, and then fun with her friends. They had allowed her to take the car for a spin on those narrow, steep roads, which is why she is smiling as she recalls her mother's look of stupor after her father agreed to her request, on the condition, however, that she return before eight to help Mom poach the lobsters for dinner. It may have been the music on the radio, or her anxiety over the cigarette that was forbidden inside the car—one of the many clauses of the paternal contract she had had to agree to in order to sit down at the wheel—because she was happy and nervous, and that may have been why she didn't see, or failed to make out, the cab of the truck coming over the brow of the hill and descending out of control and invading her lane, with its trailer and the drawing of a fish facing the car, a huge tail that sent up a spray of the dirty ice piled up on the roadside, like the wedge of a snowplow, so she didn't have time to get out of the way, she had barely come around the corner when its slightly rusty bumper was already sinking into the windshield. She caught a glimpse of the blue and white drawing of the truck's logo—a swordfish—an image that merged with the imprecise pain in her abdomen, something giving way at the height of her sternum just as she was assailed by the idea that this couldn't be happening, not that exact day, at that time, when she was only five minutes away from reaching home and helping her mother prepare dinner and laughing at Óscar's dirty jokes, perhaps meeting up alone somewhere in the snowy valley, and laughing with her friends, going for drinks with them, proud of her own silence, of how she was maturing harmlessly and the winter wasn't rough, but soft, happy, like a lemon vodka cocktail. Now, however, there was only silence around her and the oppression in her chest wouldn't cease. It was later, on the other side of the iron and the glint of glass, that she felt a shape moving, as if stroking her chin. She heard panting, and it took her a while to realize this was the sound of her own breathing. A hoarse sound, as of strangled cattle. She felt the shape shaking, moving in time to her head, forward and backward, on the passenger seat. But the impression was fleeting, and then the movement stopped. She saw her hand still clinging to the wheel, emerging from the red sleeve of her red parka. The noise of the blowtorches, followed later by the bluish gleam of a helmet, struck her as distant details, quite clearly out of reach of that hand, which was hers and yet insisted on clinging to the steering wheel. She heard orders or entreaties and then became unstuck. She stopped feeling the wheel when the chin of a man peered through the car chassis. He slipped in beside her. Other shadows maneuvered outside. When she emerged from the iron, the cold reached up to her hips. She heard more voices, imperative, solicitous, then more hushed. Somebody took her hand, and again she was surrounded by silence, until another voice, on the other side of the window, belonging to somebody not wearing a uniform or a reflective jacket but just a gown spattered with drops of blood as tiny and glistening as those of the birds Polanski abandons on the porch, said something, leaning over her. This shadow had been very near, moving around her, and was now reflected in the window of the room with the persistence of an old dream. Other silhouettes shook, too, and talked hurriedly. Now, however, it wasn't a voice, but a lament saying, "Oh, please . . . oh, please," on the other side of the blinds in that white place, where there were only tubes, saline bags, and respirators. And then nothing, a faint impression of being abandoned that started from the feet and climbed slowly, unavoidably, and yet with a smile.

7

The ringing of the phone sounds too shrill in the semidarkness of the house. The day has not begun yet, and the phone call adds a note of unnecessary urgency. The anonymous observer is not oblivious to this acoustic interruption that forces the room to disturb its internal order with a succession of imperceptible acts, beginning with the portrait of the woman, who blinks one, two, three times, accustoming her eyes to the light. Beneath her perhaps somewhat perplexed gaze, the beetle takes off from the telephone and flies over the living room with the soft hum of a fan. It leaves behind the silver cutlery, the sculpture in the form of an ostrich egg, the pages of the diary still spread out over the kitchen floor, and goes up to the second floor. It flies over the dirty pajamas, the alarm clock that has stopped at half past six, then, maneuvering like a fighter jet, dodges the cat that is dozing on the radiator and suddenly awakes and takes a swipe at it. The beetle zooms through the hallway, but nobody answers the call, so it goes up to the attic. It glides around the study, past the book-filled shelves, the discarded papers, and the open laptop, on whose plasma screensaver hangs the weightless image of an astronaut. With mechanical tenacity, the insect swings around and repeats the journey in the opposite direction. Foreseeing the cat's ambush, it stays up at the height of the lamp and, as the phone continues ringing insistently down below, passes through the bedroom, crosses the hallway, and dives down to the living room. Before folding its forewings, it mounts to the ceiling in a display of aeronautical skill that does not go unnoticed by the woman in the portrait. She squints as the beetle flutters on a level with her eyebrows. Like a helicopter, it descends toward the phone just as the red light of the answering machine starts blinking— "*I can't come to the phone right now. If you'd like to leave a message, please do so after the tone . . .*" The beetle folds its wings, and there is a beep to indicate the beginning of the message.

"*I imagine you're on the way to the clinic, but if not, forgive me for calling so early. I suppose you remember . . . today is Laura's anniversary . . . There's something else. I spoke to my lawyer yesterday. The real estate agent called him to say there's someone very interested in buying the house. They assured him that if we can reach an agreement, we should be able to resolve the matter very quickly. My lawyer will take care of all the paperwork. We need to see each other and talk. OK, I'll try and catch you later.*"

The woman in the painting returns to her initial hieratic state, fixes her gaze on the shadow of the anonymous observer, who now withdraws from the space where the pages of Laura's diary are. It could be said the text seems to have been written recently, despite the traces of humidity, faded ink, and other signs of decay, and this gives the diary a fertile elegance, as if the author of these sentences were breathing through the paper. A breath is gently expelled into the air of the living room in a combustion of oxygen only witnessed by the objects there, now silent and still, and the cat, which, sensing the movement of the observer, moves off the radiator and stealthily descends the stairs. It walks lazily, indolently, toward the kitchen, hops up onto the table, and closes its eyes. The flame of the memory of the girl writing at the living-room table one afternoon three years earlier, a blond-tobacco cigarette between her fingers, still glows green in its pupils.

She wrote with a concentrated, nervous air. She lifted her eyes from the notebook, as if seeking inspiration in the view of the garden, then in the dining room ceiling. She bit a piece of skin stuck to the nail of her thumb, then carried on writing. As she exhaled the smoke of her cigarette, the doorbell rang. She jumped in her chair. Waved her arms around in front of her face to dispel the smoke. Stood up with athletic agility and opened the window to the garden. "I'm coming!" she shouted, throwing the cigarette butt outside. Through the peephole, she recognized the silhouette of her uncle Óscar, somewhat deformed by the fisheye lens, on the doormat. She arranged her hair before opening the door.

"How's it going, Lo? Is your father in?" asked Óscar, having kissed his niece on the cheek.

"He's not back yet, and my mother's in town, shopping. I don't know when she'll be back."

"Do re mi, do re fa," crooned the man jokingly.

His tanned skin heightened an impression of adventure or risk in his appearance. He wore a photographer's vest with lots of pockets. Under his arm, he carried a motorcyclist's gleaming, black helmet. The helmet reminded Laura of the head of a large, outer-space beetle.

"Were you studying?" he pointed at the notebook open on the table.

Laura hesitated for a moment, went around the table, and closed the notebook.

"No, actually I was just writing," she gestured vaguely, "things of mine."

The man smiled with interest. Sat down on the blue sofa.

"Are you not going to invite your uncle to a beer?"

Laura left the room for a few moments, her walk attracting the man's gaze. She returned with a Keler beer, an iced glass, and a bowl of peanuts. She let her uncle serve himself. She drank from a carton of pineapple juice.

Óscar sipped the beer while contemplating his niece. He thought she was getting much older, but this distance, far from separating them, brought them closer together, since age does not divide people but in the end draws them together—Laura was a woman. He wondered whether to adopt a paternal or confidential tone with her. He opted for the latter. It went better with his theory of age, and it was time to treat Laura like she deserved, as an equal.

"Were you really writing? When you feel bad, it's good to write. I used to do it, you know. Before I got into photojournalism, I mean. I also wrote things of mine, as you say, dreams, desires, stuff like that, in these tiny, spiral-bound notebooks, with cramped writing . . . I wrote most of all when I felt bad. They've probably gotten lost during some move or other. But it's good to do it, really it is. I even wrote poems, can you believe it? Your uncle Óscar, a poet . . ."

Laura smiled in disbelief.

"Really?" she asked.

"Really, I swear," said Óscar, kissing his thumb. "I was a very shy boy, you know, and fell in love with all the girls my age, all of them. I wrote them the most heartfelt, sincere poems." He gazed at the ceiling in a gesture of concentration. "I wonder if I can remember . . . ah, yes! I wrote these verses with a blond girl in mind. See what you think." He raised his beer glass and recited in a stifled voice, "And you will return forever to your fields of oblivion / and I will be left with the ashen smell of your hair / how slow and piercing your footsteps echo in my heart / I wonder what moon I will lick my wounds under now . . ."

He forced a declamatory silence.

"What do you think?" he asked.

Laura observed him, a little lost in thought.

"It's nice . . . ," she looked at the window to the garden and allowed the words to sound again in her head. "I like that bit about the ashen smell of your hair, and the moon and wounds . . . I don't know why I write. It makes me feel good, I suppose that's all . . . it gives me some relief," she said, perching on the armrest of the sofa. "I could never write something as pretty as that."

The man smiled, unable to avoid a paternal gesture, just as he couldn't help noticing her lips painted with

Chinese red lipstick. In front of him was not his niece but an athletic woman, worthy of being contemplated at a distance that precluded any kind of filial bond, the way one looks at a beautiful, desirable, innocent woman. He nodded while at the same time framing the girl with his fingers.

"You certainly look beautiful," he said, closing one eye, watching her through his fingers, framed in the imaginary viewfinder of a camera. "How young you are, Lo, how young, there's still so much you don't know."

"Nobody ever wrote me such nice verses."

The man pressed the shutter of his camera. Thought it would have made a magnificent photo, a portrait of plenitude.

"No, Laura, those verses are terrible. You deserve something a lot better. You're a real woman now, just look at you, I'll bet there are tons of boys jumping up around you, like puppies. Though I don't suppose they write poems as bad as mine, boys nowadays don't write poetry, right? Besides, you only write when you're unhappy. And you're not unhappy, are you?"

"I'm just a silly girl," she said with a frown. Her lower lip began to tremble. "A silly girl," she repeated, on the verge of tears.

"What makes you say that?"

"A very silly girl," she said again, her face in her hands.

Her shoulders trembled rhythmically. The man embraced her. Between hiccups, she told her uncle all about her amorous disenchantment with Antonio. Sitting next to him on the sofa, Laura confessed her solitude, the bitter experience of feeling used and betrayed for the first

166

time. Laying her forehead on his chest, she said she felt very alone at home, with those parents of hers, enclosed like fish in their respective fishbowls, each gaping away alone, without paying attention to anything or anybody; she talked of her fear of failing her exams, of disappointing her father, the university professor, and her mother, who was so good, so quiet, so focused on her exotic dishes. Everything, in short, was a black block that weighed down on her chest and stopped her from breathing properly, a maze she couldn't get out of, which is why she wrote, but she still kept feeling this black block on top of her chest and couldn't get rid of it. Her uncle wiped her face with a handkerchief he produced from one of the multiple pockets on his photographer's vest, dried her tears, and kissed her on the cheek, near her lip. He felt the girl's chest shaking against his own, pumping the cleanest blood imaginable, the blood of all horses stampeding, of all thoroughbreds there have ever been, the boiling blood of a volcano, the sap of a primitive fruit tree, the tree of good and evil, a ripe substance now pushing to overflow all banks, like the systole and diastole of a desire it was no longer possible to repress, and he detected, very close to him, the scent of freshly squeezed lemons given off by his niece's body, impregnating the fabric of her T-shirt; her gentle breath, which smelled of a mixture of pineapple juice and tobacco, issued a tender, voluptuous invitation, so he took her by the shoulders and brushed aside her hair in order to search out the bottom of her eyes and say in the voice of a radio presenter, "You mustn't worry, I'm here to help you. Don't be afraid." And it seemed to him that his voice sounded a little shrill, as if he were afraid or lying, so he coughed to clear his throat and repeated, in a polished voice now, without a hint of doubt, "Don't be afraid, please."

Laura nodded while rubbing her eyes. She let her uncle stroke the back of her neck and pressed her cheek against his neck, just as she had dreamed so often. And as happens in certain dreams, everything was very simple, without blunders or hesitations; she just let herself go, let herself be cradled by that wise, silky voice, the touch of fingers on her neck, behind her ears, then around her shoulders, moving around the nape of her neck and her dragon tattoo, long fingers that traced her skin and now climbed up the back of her skull, pressing electric buttons concealed beneath her scalp, like acupuncture points.

"Laura . . ."

"What?" she replied.

She heard the voice repeating her name very close to her ears and felt her legs tremble a little when Óscar's lips sought out her own, but she did not reject the advance, rather she succumbed to a desire she had only ever expressed in solitary yearnings, while stroking her sex in the bath and discovering without surprise the same shuddering between her thighs, except that now there was another body, a pair of hands, a mouth, and skin, all very different from Antonio's bony, angled body; this was the body of a man, an energetic, comfortable shape emitting a warmth that took her in and carried her off, which is why she allowed herself to fall back slowly onto the sofa, her uncle kissing her on the neck, and she detected the scent of a sport cologne, acidic sweat, a man's smell replacing Antonio's, which struck her now as rancid, the smell of old ashes, a wet dog, and Óscar's body was replacing Antonio's, which moved away, getting smaller and smaller, coming off like the slough of a snake, from his head to his toes, slowly to begin with—she watched him stagger along with his leather bracelets, his black T-shirt, and samurai ponytail toward the end of an alley that could be the darkest bottom of his own shoes—and then more quickly, seemingly pushed by an invisible force as she advanced in the exploration of Óscar's body, so solid, that of a grown man, and felt his strong hands grabbing her gently, molding themselves to the shape of her tiny swimmer's breasts, then she gazed into the bottom of those eyes, so close to her they were transformed into the single eye of a Cyclops, and deep inside watched Antonio leave without moving, inert, like a straw man that has just been thrown into the current of a river.

Polanski half-opens its eyes, and outside, on the other side of the window, the figure of the man, looking slightly larger on account of his warm clothes, moves around. His actions are meant to be energetic, but all he does is move in the cold of the morning, which forces him to walk back and forth in front of the door with short steps, like a bird. He rubs his hands together on the roadside, but stops when he discovers an orange sign with a telephone number under the words "FOR SALE." The placard bears the name of a real estate agent from the capital. The logo shows the needle-like silhouette of the Chrysler Building in New York. Somebody has gone to the trouble of using a ladder to stick the sign on one of the upstairs windows of the house. The advertisement is absurd, pointless. Who on earth could see that for-sale sign? Nobody, except for the black kites. Somebody must have put it there the day before, when he was out walking. He must call Ana and demand an explanation. She should have asked his permission before agreeing to a sign like that. He must write *Call Ana re sign* on a sticky note and put it on the door of the fridge.

He tests the edge of a frozen puddle with the tip of his boot. Seen from the kitchen window, it could be said he is reflecting on something, but in fact, all he's doing is shaking; he hasn't had breakfast, and his swollen fingers beat inside his gloves, the inside of his head is full of cold air, and it isn't a pleasant sensation but rather an icy weariness that keeps him stuck to the puddle. He goes over his ingestion of food in the previous forty-eight hours. He imagines the chief nurse screwing up her nose, as if detecting a bad smell, when the scales confirm the excess weight of the university professor and renowned art critic who recently seems to have adopted the habit of coming to dialysis with a couple of extra pounds. He'll have no choice but to admit that he drank too much water the night before; the pizza, Laura's diary, the subsequent lack of tobacco—he had to calm his nerves somehow, so he drank until he was sated. But now, as he detaches himself from the puddle and walks back and forth along the pavement, he's lugging around all that liquid, and he feels it accumulating in his fingers, and also his ankles, and eyelids. He checks his watch; it's already after seven thirty. He raises his hand with impatience at the oncoming car, and the headlights illuminate the holes in the unpaved road in bursts. The taxi driver's look is framed in the rearview mirror. "We're a bit pressed for time today," he says, and the man nods, a little befuddled by the blasting warmth coming from the car's heating. On the radio, two men discuss the government's foreign policy. The taxi driver shakes his head and clicks his tongue, leans toward the radio and insults one of the program participants. His features are framed in the rearview mirror—a pair of rural eyebrows, a frown, small eyes. The broad, red nape of his neck is half-hidden by the collar of his wool sweater. As usual, the car stops at Jeremías's post. His figure can just be made out behind the steamed-up glass, seated next to a thermos. When he sees them, he passes the newspaper through the car window. The man says good morning and drops a coin into his chapped hand, but Jeremías simply grunts in reply, pulls his cap down over his head, and goes back to his little room in short jumps. The taxi driver traces a mocking smile in the rearview mirror. The car heads for the highway, and the gas station disappears behind them. Perhaps he should have asked Jeremías about the accident, he must know what happened. He saw him bend down next to one of the windows. He must know what became of the car's occupants. Two? Three? How many people were traveling in the car? Perhaps in the last few hours there has been a multiple organ donation and somebody, like him, will receive a kidney, a liver, or a heart. "Jeremías gets crazier every day," says the taxi driver, pointing to his temple.

The lights of dawn sparkle on the frosted ground. From the fallow fields emerges a mist that clouds the early morning with a suggestion of tundra. There are pairs of rooks pecking at the fields, and long puddles covered in a thin layer of ice. The sky grows light timidly, imprecisely, until the slightly polar clarity sketches the outlines of houses in the city, the white smoke of several chimneys, the first garbage trucks. There are people in the street now—they come out of their front doors, bent double against the cold; there are pedestrians waiting at bus stops and others being swallowed down by the entrance to the metro; a homeless person walled in by cardboard; and a man walking his brick-red dachshund in the park. They stop at a traffic light, and a girl walks past in front of them. He feels a sudden dizziness. He sits up to take a better look—the coat with the large collar, the medium-length hair, the beauty spot on her cheek, the student's backpack. The vision of the girl introduces a misalignment into his perception—the gesture of a painter taking a step back and squinting to gaze at the canvas—and he is on the verge of saying "Laura." The taxi driver turns down the radio.

"Pretty, huh?" he says, keeping his eyes on the girl, who has already reached the opposite sidewalk and is rounding the corner of a building covered in scaffolding.

"What was that?"

"The girl . . . you know what I mean," he draws a pair of hips in the air, "a real beauty."

"I thought it was somebody I knew."

"All cats are gray in the dark, right?" says the taxi driver, winking in the rearview mirror.

The windows are misted up.

"It's very hot in here," says the man, as if talking to himself.

The taxi driver shrugs his shoulders, turns down the temperature, but turns up the radio. The presenter states that the world is immersed in fear, that's the main driving force, fear, and nothing else, and one day we will know the true causes of international terrorism, which will be purely economic, as history clearly shows; but another voice declares that the crux of the matter resides in the impression of an immediate threat and in knowing who is creating the problem, who profits from the fear, because fear, he maintains, is not free, but just the opposite; a third voice, however, remarks that this is infamy, because fear feeds on itself, without interruption, without measure; a fourth voice attempts to refute this hypothesis, and the debate descends into an incomprehensible discussion syncopated by voices cutting each other off. The presenter appeals for calm and proceeds to encourage the listeners to phone in and express their opinions. "Because you, dear listener," he says before going to commercial, "are what the news is really about."

The taxi driver turns off the radio while dodging a line of cars. A local bus gets in their way, so he brakes suddenly. He honks the horn by banging on the center of the steering wheel.

The image of the girl was not a mistake, but a grimace of imagination or memory. He smiles on thinking of the face the taxi driver would have made if he'd informed him that the girl who just passed in front of them was not the silhouette of a pretty, young woman, or his lover, but a joke, nothing more, a joke of his dead daughter's. He hasn't managed to establish a chronological link to imbue these events with meaning but has ended up qualifying them as a private joke. They used to disconcert him, but now they put him on a state of alert.

Having read Laura's diary after the morning news failed to send him to sleep, he took a bottle of mineral water and went up to the second floor. He wasn't searching for anything, he just kept walking and gazing at the frieze of the walls. Everything was still as it was supposed to be, with the slightly spectral quietude of a domestic museum—the teddy bears, the schoolbooks, the parka, the red spine of the photo album. He picked it up and sat on the edge of the bed. There were the postcards Óscar had sent her from all over the world—the Brooklyn Bridge, the Twin Towers, the spectral lights of Osaka, Tlatelolco Plaza in Mexico City, a suburb in South Africa, the Inca ruins of Machu Picchu, and Ankara, and St. Petersburg. He stopped at the image of a water buffalo. This postcard had been sent from Bangkok. He took it out of the album and read the text. *You see I don't forget you. Even when I'm very far away. You'd like this country a lot. I bet you a ride on my bike this arrives in time for your birthday. Love you, Óscar.* He drained his bottle of mineral water and tried to sleep. He could feel the sparrows chirping on the roof.

Perhaps it's only right that Ana should know about the diary, should read what he himself has read. It is her daughter. He weighs up the possibility of showing it to her censored; he would only need to hide a few parts, the most insidious references, in particular the salacious evidence of Laura and Óscar's relations. That way, Ana would be accessing the diary of a teenager, because that's what it is, no more, no less, a text, like any other, written

174

to express her insecurities, disappointments, trouble communicating, questions to which there is never an answer—the diary of a young girl. He wonders what would hurt Ana the most. Perhaps all he would achieve is to cause her posthumous, gratuitous pain. After all, it wasn't addressed to her, but to him; the diary is his discovery, his secret, his joke. He tells himself he should protect Ana from this revelation. He wonders what hurts him the most, and in fact it is his own disappearance, his absence, or worse still, the references to an image that is very similar to the shadow of an anonymous observer, a neutral, floating attention that judges everything with dispassionate curiosity. That was him, a deaf presence. And that's the most revealing thing, even more, perhaps, than the image of a morbid passion—Laura and Óscar making love in a wheat field, secretly kissing on the porch—which is something he can accept without argument, because, when it comes down to it, and this was the painful joke, he didn't know Laura. He knew nothing about her. Though he also knew now that his daughter had been happy.

The intermittent sound of a horn brings him back to the image of the cold sidewalks. He examines his heart, but only feels a vague sadness.

"We are definitely going to be late today," declares the taxi driver.

The traffic lights change color. The car continues down the city's main avenue, finally gets past the traffic, and enters a tunnel that leads to a large plaza near the clinic. He pays for the journey, leaves the car, and heads for the revolving door of the medical center. He is greeted

by the piped music—*Raindrops keep falling on my head*—
and anticipates the salty taste of saline in his mouth. He
changes in the cubicle and comes out in a pair of beige-
colored pajamas. The room smells of bandages and iodine.
From the sofa, Ángel raises his eyebrows in greeting while
the ward manager leans in toward the scales. She screws
up her nose. "I can't believe that someone like you should
behave like a little child," she says, while at the same time
jotting down his weight in her notebook. "You're more
than four and a half pounds over today." He stretches out
his arm on the venipuncture table. Sara's latex-gloved
fingers explore his fistula indecisively, pressing down on
the gaps that are still free, between his tendon and his
muscle. She doesn't tell jokes today, she is nervous. Or she
seems to be, and this is not a good sign. It could be said
he feels his veins shrinking under his skin. He holds his
breath and counts to ten. He doesn't close his eyes. He
is just preparing himself for the worst, when the needle
forces its way through skin as hard as lemon rind.

8

He should have realized it wasn't going to be a good day at the clinic, especially when Ángel pointed in the direction of the chocolate-colored armchair somebody had placed under the window. A pigeon was delousing itself on the windowsill. It was a dirty, anxious bird, but it wasn't the pigeon that had attracted his attention, and Ángel gestured again, this time with his jaw, at Tere's armchair, which was still empty, slightly tilted back, like the chair at a dentist's, next to the machine's loose cables. He quizzed his companion with his eyes. Ángel hadn't seen the girl in the waiting room, and certainly not at the venipuncture table, he was absolutely sure about that. A woman brought the breakfast trays as usual. They watched her movements, how she served the decaffeinated coffee, the rolls spread with butter and jam. She handed out the breakfasts without stopping at Tere's place. This time, all Ángel did was screw up his nose. The man sipped his coffee greedily. After a while, the nurses filed out of their room. They formed a perplexed, silent group. The ward manager stepped forward and asked for their attention. She stared at the floor tiles, as if pondering the firmness of the ground under her feet. Perhaps she wasn't sure how to talk to them and was remembering her medical training courses, though she must have confronted similar situations before. She seemed to opt for the most professional approach. She shuffled her clogs and looked up at them, but her eyes, absorbed by the tiles on the wall, seemed to fly over the top of them, attentive to some object moving behind them. Tere's mother had phoned first thing. She had found her early that morning, on the floor, next to a broken glass, perhaps she had been thirsty, had filled a glass with water in the kitchen, and on the way back to her room, had collapsed. Her mother had tried in vain to resuscitate her and then called for help. The ambulance didn't take long to arrive, but all the medical team could do was certify her death. Tere had died of cardiac arrest; her heart, while young, must have had some congenital condition. In the absence of conclusive proof, this was the likeliest hypothesis; this is what the nephrologists had told her. She *could* say that Tere hadn't suffered, she probably hadn't even had time to realize she was dying. She pointed toward the other nurses, they were all deeply affected, as was the medical team, which given the patient's young age, had, from the start of her illness, followed her case with special interest. A funeral would be held in the clinic's chapel sometime in the coming days. Her eyes stopped wandering all over the room and glazed over. They, she said, should not lose hope; when they least expected it, they could receive a call from the Transplant Coordination Center to inform them that they were the recipients of a kidney. Every month, dozens of such operations were carried out.

The donation of an organ was a gift that could arrive at any moment, possibly long before they imagined, so they should be ready to receive it in the best possible of conditions. "We will all remember Tere with great affection," she said, gazing at her team of nurses. She may have been waiting for one of them to corroborate her words. There was a silence that demanded to be broken. Ambrosio coughed loudly when the nurses left the room. The rhythmic sound of the machines evoked a group of beached dinghies. Encouraged, perhaps, by the tone the chief nurse's words had taken on, the Jehovah's witness suggested they pray together for the girl's soul, but nobody seconded his proposal. Marcela's face was contorted into an expression of mourning. Next to her, Ángel sighed. He hoped that, just as the ward manager had suggested, Tere hadn't suffered. In the light coming from the window, her armchair resembled an old shoe; on the other side, the pigeon remained quiet, dozing on the sill.

His forearm throbbed, lacerated by needle marks. Sara had taken a while to find the fistula, and now the pain spread under the surgical tape like a jellyfish sting, but this sensation seemed to absolve him, and it extended up through the tube that kept him connected to the machine and through the vision of his blood warming the plastic, being sucked toward the membrane. He was still there, like the armchair, like the pigeon, he hadn't gone, and this idea kept his spirits up, so he breakfasted with gusto. He couldn't concentrate on reading the newspaper, so he amused himself by gazing at the light coming from the fluorescent tubes on the ceiling. He imagined Tere, small, large-headed, in the slightly obscene light of the tubes, her tawny-owl face pressed against a green carpet in the darkness of a dining room, dressed in a pink nightdress, her legs positioned as if ready to jump. Her thighs were chubby and very white. She had lost her glasses in the fall, and out of the broken lenses poured water that soaked the linoleum. He saw her mother enter the dining room and kneel down next to her. She covered her thighs with the edge of her nightdress. She squeezed her face, pinched her cheeks. Stood up, moved away from the body, walked around the room a little, and raised her arms to the sky, like a silent film actress. Somewhere in the house, possibly in the hallway, a phone rang, but nobody picked up.

When he opened his eyes, he was overwhelmed by an impression of distance. The ceiling seemed very high, a mute, insolent color. He saw a nurse passing through the air, which appeared to be made of the same matter as fever, but she did so in a way he'd never seen before, moving effortlessly, like an astronaut, while that phone kept ringing in the hallway. Ángel slept with his eyelids half open and his face stuck to the pillow. A glob of saliva was gathering in the corner of his mouth. He felt the absurd certainty that something serious was about to happen; he didn't want anything bad to happen to Ángel, he wanted to say something, to warn him, while the phone kept ringing somewhere in the room, and not even the nurse, walking past him again on her way to the corridor, seemed to notice. So he made an effort to lift himself up on his elbows. "Ángel, wake up!" he shouted, but he had the impression his words vanished like air from a spray bottle. He was aware that he really could go, like Tere, and that it was going to happen very quickly. The impression of light dizziness turned, little by little, into slow-motion vertigo and a slope it was extremely easy to slide down, weightlessly, while his words disintegrated into particles of vapor. The impression of alarm subsided, and the rings of the phone sounded ever more distant. He felt himself letting go. He could no longer hear the sound of the phone. *How easy it is to die*, he thought, and it was agreeable to feel himself being overwhelmed by this comfortable insensitivity. It was simple, too. There were no literary pleonasms, no philosophical nauseas, no rhetoric of anguish. It was as commonplace as turning off the mechanisms on a machine one by one, releasing the cables without nostalgia or Tenebrae services. It was pleasant, reassuring. And, above all, peaceful.

An intense cramp brought him back to consciousness, a knife penetrating his leg on the back of his knee and climbing up the inside of his thigh to the root of his buttock. The process repeated on the other leg with the precision of a scalpel. He howled in pain, rigid, between the footrest and headrest, and the light from the fluorescent tube fell suddenly onto his eyelids, but he couldn't focus on anything except for the figure of Sara moving back and forth across his field of vision among the little lights jumping from the center of his forehead and then over the oxygen mask somebody clamped against his chin. He could see Sara moving between disks of light, violet flowers, islets of blood plasma. He felt elastic bands around his ears and the air tickling his nostrils. It was a pleasant lightness that entered his lungs and cleaned his field of vision. He noticed the figure of another nurse. Saw her inject some liquid into the saline tube. Still half asleep, Ángel watched what was going on. His cheek was furrowed by the wrinkle on his pillow. This detail calmed him down, as did the glob of saliva that had clotted in the corner of his mouth. Sara kept on watching him from the foot of his armchair, her hands on her hips. He couldn't be sure whether it was a look of relief or reproach, but little by little his leg muscles relaxed, and he felt himself going down, or up, effortlessly changing place from some previous location, until he was again sitting comfortably in the imitation-leather armchair. He grabbed the chair and took a deep breath, though it sounded more like a snort. The ward manager took off the oxygen mask. She smiled, then pursed her lips. *You see now?* she seemed to be saying with that expression, and he nodded in exhaustion, gripping the armrests, and kept nodding with relief after all the nurses had moved off down the hallway.

He had to get used to being there again, to fall back in time with the *glup-glup* of the machines. The sound struck him as reassuring, domestic, like the hum of a fridge. He needed to click his tongue again, detect the salty taste of saline, move his toes, blink. Such trivial actions confirmed he had returned to a halfway point between pain and imperturbability. Nobody could live breathing pain, not for long, while imperturbability, on the other hand, invited you to settle into it, leave everything behind so as to be rocked in a place without time or space, always one step away from salvation and beatitude, but also from corruption and tedium.

He wondered where he was now. Even if he wanted to, he wouldn't be able to escape from the room, nor could he accept the possibility of spending the rest of his life in this position, adapting himself to the rhythm of the dialyzer, anticipating the symptoms of a fainting fit without return. He stayed alert, but the rest of the morning passed without incident. The light of the fluorescent tubes heightened the impression of a prolonged sleep, as if the very air in the room had acquired a liquid, salty consistency. From the street could be heard the sound of car horns, which seemed strangely in time with the beeps and warning lights on the machines the nurses had already started disconnecting with all the hullabaloo of a gambling den. He'd have given anything to be the first to be disconnected from the tubes. In fact, anybody would have wanted to be first, but he'd come to dialysis twenty minutes late, so now he had no choice but to watch the other patients already peeling themselves off their armchairs and walking weightlessly and noiselessly toward the scales. He felt Ángel's hand stroke his shoulder. "Take care," he said, dragging his feet. He attempted to relax. Time seemed to dilate, heavy and somnolent, in the room. The machine continued pumping his blood through the pistons. If nobody stopped the process, the machine would carry on purifying his blood until it turned it into a very fine sheet. He considered the absurd and terrifying possibility of the nurses going off and leaving him there, all forgotten. How long would he be able to last? He would have to shout to make himself heard. But that could never happen, at least not while the pigeon in the window, dirty and complacent, continued delousing itself. There was something insulting in the insipid gluttony with which it searched for parasites among its feathers. And yet there was also something reassuring, like the signals emitted by a marker buoy at sea. The cleaning staff spread disinfectant over the floor, and the smell was not all that unpleasant, rather it struck him as reminiscent of chlorinated water. Finally, he felt himself being detached from the tubes. Sara performed the operation at great speed, as if wanting to make up for the needle pokes. She led him by the arm to the nurses' station. They took his blood pressure. He should eat as soon as he got home, they said. A very young doctor entered the room. He looked like an intern, or a resident. The head of the nephrology department had already been informed about his mishap. He leaned toward him as if searching for a sign deep within his eyes. Asked him how he felt. He didn't know what to say, except that he felt very weak, and when he said this, he had the impression his voice was a very thin wire. "The truth is I just want to go home. That's all," he added. The doctor wrote something on a piece of paper. Sara took his blood pressure again and measured his pulse. Then they let him go. He got dressed and went back through the corridors, the elevator, the revolving door of the clinic, but couldn't recognize the tune of the piped music, which seemed to emanate from the walls of the building, or the fresh air beating against the corner of the taxi stand. He got in the car without the driver even realizing it. He closed the door, and the driver jumped in his seat. He turned toward him, between the seats, looking very pale, as if he'd just seen an apparition. He recovered from his fright by tuning into the radio. The man was convinced he had become transparent.

During the day, his skin has stuck to his cheekbones, acquiring an eroded pallor. The door to the remote possibility of a visit having been closed, the mirror shows him the image of a man with ruffled hair and an urgent look. It's an image that repels him, fleeting, glimpsed out of the corner of his eye. He reaches the shadow of the entryway and drops his parka, gloves, and keys. He has the impression he has gotten back from a long journey. He has closed the door, and everything has been left on the other side; the faces, words, and fears no longer belong to him, he has left them outside, like a scattering of objects tossed into a ditch. The weariness of his figure in the mirror is proof that he is safe, as if the fact of having returned home excused him from weighing up other uncertainties. Polanski mews at his feet, he feels the cat's claws digging into his ankle. Limping, he walks toward the kitchen. He rids himself of the animal by moving it aside with the inside of his boot, as if pushing a ball, and the cat retreats toward the kitchen, narrowing its green, resentful eyes at the abruptly slender figure of the man now leaning against the doorjamb, as if drunk. He can still feel the points of light jumping off his forehead, like a school of silvery fry leaping onto the table and moving through the space of the kitchen, above the cat, though the animal seems not to realize and focuses its gaze, fixed and horizontal like the surface of a pond, on the man. He has the impression he is an evaporated body, transfixed by air, the body of a traveler who despite having reached the arrival gate at an airport, is unable to adjust to the new surroundings. He should buy a blood pressure monitor, he has to jot this down on a sticky note, write

Buy blood pressure monitor, and stick the message to the door of the fridge. He forces himself to eat—a portion of mold-encrusted Bimbo bread and a few slices of cheese. He rescues a cup of cold coffee from the thermos and adds three spoonfuls of sugar. It smells of cold ashes. He wonders when he made this coffee. A sip is more than enough; it is, quite simply, awful. He curses himself for not having any Coke in the pantry, so he forces himself to drink the coffee. He accompanies the purgative with a handful of sweet peanuts bought from Jeremías. He tells himself he should revive the habit of bread and eat real bread, crusty, freshly made; there are towns in the valley where you can find loaves straight out of *Don Quixote*. He imagines freshly baked bread, crunchy, real. He no longer perceives the lights that were jumping off his forehead like sparks from a grindstone; they have disappeared into the air of the kitchen, and everything acquires more precise limits around him. He again feels the force of gravity, the weight of his shoulders, of his legs, the weight of his teeth, as well. Polanski mews loudly now. The reproach doesn't pass unnoticed; he forgot to give the cat its ration of Whiskas before leaving the house. On opening the fridge, he is assailed by the rancid smell of leftover food. From behind a few soggy mandarins, he extracts the can of pet food. He scrapes it clean, depositing the lumps into the plastic bowl. He pats the cat's head in a conciliatory fashion.

"Wet food again, Polanski," he says. His voice retains a wiry consistency. He notices the cat has grown quite fat in the last few months, in fact, it has the hairy belly of a circus lion hanging off it; he, on the other hand, has grown a lot thinner. He forces himself to digest his meager lunch until he feels his blood flowing and his body acquiring a definitive consistency, similar to that of the wood of the table. Now his hand is his hand, his chest is his chest, his legs are his legs, his gums are his gums, too, Laura's diary is Laura's diary.

On the side table, the answering machine is blinking. The red light seems to demand his attention with a wink of urgency. He halfheartedly presses the listen button. Ana wants to talk to him, as soon as possible, she adds details concerning the arrangements for selling the house, some of which require his approval. The answering machine mechanism stops, but the red light keeps blinking, the recorded voice announcing another message, so he again presses the listen button. The machine reads out Óscar's number. His voice does not conceal his concern or tiredness, though the tone is jovial. "Hello, Gabriel, I'm back. This trip was really worthwhile; you should see where I've been . . . to the promised land. Ana called me to say she's been trying to talk to you for several days. It appears she's on the verge of closing a deal to sell the house, but she can't locate you. Where on earth have you been? I called the clinic, and a nurse told me you gave them a real fright. You just can't be left alone. Are you all right? If you don't return this call, I'll come around to pick you up tomorrow at noon. We can have lunch together. My treat. Take care."

He imagines Óscar tanned by the sun of Singapore or Timbuktu, with his camera still hanging around his neck, his plane tickets, his passport, his luggage still unpacked, sleepless and dirty in the middle of his room, collapsing into the armchair to have a snooze while images of deserted beaches, palm trees, and coral reefs peel away from his retinas like fish scales. He imagines him right now next to the phone, snoring loudly, crushed by the fatigue of his journey.

He climbs the stairs slowly, feeling calm at long last, as if the silence now filling the house had fallen lightly on his shoulders, oblivious to the presence of the anonymous observer who walks alongside him, accompanying him. He is grateful for the solitude of his bedroom. He turns his body to the wall, and the mattress groans beneath his hip. He folds his arm under the pillow. He is grateful for the proximity of objects, is calmed by the wall, the glass of water covered in bubbles, the pills, the alarm clock. Everything is there, within arm's reach. He feels the warm shape of the cat nestling between his feet.

Perhaps everything consists in remaining very still in the light and, like a skin beneath the sheets, breathing in the air that comes with a slight fragrance of saltpeter, since the sea, though distant, can be felt here, reaching all the way from the other side of the mountains, the same direction from which storms choose to cover the valley. From that direction comes the air, movement, a desire for action, a panting for life that issues forth in bursts from the most isolated depths, but also from the closest vicinity. This certainty comes to him at times when everything around him takes on an elegance more real than reality itself, if such a thing is admissible or even imaginable once the moment has passed. When *that* happens, space takes on its exact, overwhelming dimension. Reality reveals itself with a smoothing of edges. And then something wonderful occurs. Radical surprise, the deepest Assumption. But *that* doesn't happen right now.

If the succubus of his bad dreams were to say to him, "Make a wish," he would ask to be able to mold himself to the geological quietude of stones. He manages to evoke the shape of a rock, like a tortoise shell, an eons-old stone, a smooth shape a passerby could lie down on in order to regain his strength. He would like to be a smooth, onion-colored rock, a rock that stays in the sun, on the other side of the undergrowth, hidden from the passerby who in order to discover it would have to leave the path and go in the direction of that sun glinting through the leaves and sparkling on the chalky surface with inclement whiteness—a rock. Quite simply. He can feel the morning light warming the lichen-covered surface, which is coated in frost from the cold of night, then the heat of that sun now turning in the vault of heaven, having warmed the earth in its ascent. He could feel around its rugged, prehistoric-animal surface, the first geological layer, until he reached its inner nooks and crannies where very primitive organisms move, articulated insects, tiny spiders the size of a pinhead, secluded wrinkles, cobwebs, crusts, acorn caps, fragments of pine nuts, brief putrefactions, microscopic excrescences of a hidden, silent life. Somewhere warm and dark, like a nest.

A wish, no more. And no less. Perhaps everything consists in allowing oneself to be swayed by the to-and-fro of a comfortable insensitivity, rocked by a halfhearted melody that presumes, and no doubt anticipates, the worst forms of abandonment, though at first sight this is all it seems, a dull ballad protecting but anaesthetizing one's last defenses, the rock-a-bye baby of a distant voice that rings again in the ears after one abandons oneself to the weight of one's body, and how pleasant it is then to settle into the law of gravity and to unresistingly witness one's own sinking on a surface already molded to the shape of one's body; the rock-a-bye baby on the treetop, the voice of the sirens, a sweet tidbit dissolved in the serum of memory, because deep down it's a question of forgetting one's own impulses, the hidden springs of resistance, the forgotten first school notebook, the teatime of rewards and punishments, the self-esteem, until, at a certain point of abandonment, it is no more than the precarious melody of a children's song reduced to nonsense, something that ends up disappearing and leaving in its place the sound of vulgar hammering, syncopated life.

He half-opens his eyes. Within arm's reach, the lamp pours soft devastation over the pearly gray wall, whose surface is reminiscent of the surface of a very distant planet. There is the glass of water covered in bubbles, like a reminder, the pills patiently counted out, one by one, some thirty barbiturates and sedatives in all different colors and sizes, rescued from the psychiatric pharmacopeia Ana kept in the bathroom cabinet; there are white ones, pink ones, yellow ones, green and blue ones, all in a pile he would be incapable of picking up in the palm of his hand without provoking the predictable, penultimate scene, ridiculous, a little pathetic for any inexperienced suicidal individual—bending down, on all fours, feeling around on the carpet, then beneath the bed skirt, to recover half a dozen colored pills. To say goodbye against nothing and nobody, just an act confirming the impossibility of continuing to heed the exhortation of the wind coming from the north, that longing, that remote jubilation that chooses the same direction as storms. Because that is the point: not to return. He gazes at his bare feet, a sky-blue color. The feet of a dead man. The cat doesn't realize it's resting between the feet of a dead man who is considering shoving a fistful of pills down his throat to ease the passage and washing them down with a swig of water. The purpose of this act is not to recover the lost object of desire, since there is no desire, just a pure act carried out from the very heart of desire, just as right now he feels the heat coming off the cat's body between his feet. That's what this is about. He hates psychiatric superstitions. Objects are superfluous, and he hates his feet. He has always hated them. His hands, as well. Is this a speck of desire? But he's been down this tunnel, there and back, too many times, he is familiar with the nooks and crannies, the false doors, the mirrors, games, fragments reflecting a light that only exists in a desire that is about to run out; they are only grimaces putting off the revelation, the definitive proof that this is everything. Desire makes its appearance, and it leaves. He has rehearsed the comedy of departure so many times that were it not for the fact that he loves the light, just the idea of reaching a genuine door would seem childish to him. This is clearly paradoxical when his hand is hesitating between sorting the pills by size—perhaps the smallest first, then the large ones—or by color—first the pink and yellow ones, then the green, lastly the blue—and he only has to stretch out his hand, empty the bottle of pills onto his palm, and shove the pills down his throat; there is no desire, just an act that should leave no room for doubt, and certainly not for the luminous nightmare of regret once the pills are heading down his esophagus, the succubus doubled up with laughter, clinging to its sides, on seeing his gesture of fright, so grotesque. It is just an impulse that neither seeks a solution nor aims to—that handful of colored pills, that glass of water. A capitulation. He recalls the sentence spoken so many times at Laura's funeral, and later in the cemetery. "We are nothing," they said. It has to be a willful, affirmative gesture, because in the end it's about doing away with doubts that equate light with that trivial, ultimately melancholic gesture. For this, a well-aimed desire like a stone or a handful of wet earth is necessary, something concrete that does not belong to the world of mist where everything is comfortable, vague, and uniform, an impulse that is defined in opposition to light and shadow, something real, consistent, a yes, or a no, a stone, a shout, a gesture of disillusion, since deep down, in the end, everything shelters a direction. And yet he loves golden sunlight, that light that brightens wine in bottles, the green, unmoving ray like a piece of fruit in a still life, a cracked lemon, the wrinkled skin of a quince, the light that brings out the quality of earth, or toasted sand, in the skin; he loves the slightly old light of 25-watt bulbs, the milky light of wintry skies turned orange by that other light coming from the street lamps, which bounces off the wet pavements like mandarin segments, the light emerging from the coldest, humblest puddles, inhabited by invertebrates; he loves the jovial light of spring, which is a luminous river of promises lit on the green of gardens and on the hips of girls who allow themselves to be kissed in those gardens, that light that falls on the heads of all the pedestrians in the street—whom he sees and others may not see, or perhaps they do, it's impossible to know—and ignites a tremulous light on their crowns, the same light that cleans the March sky with the glint of a frozen prism, and the sapphire light of May on a clear sky like a worn piece of blue silk that anticipates the arrival of summer, when the light will absorb the pale lime of all walls and solitary stones and abandoned rocks in dried riverbeds, the whitewashed light in eyes that chars memory or fixes it forever in a childish gesture, such as throwing a stone onto the surface of a river, or seeing the first steps of a girl in a garden surrounded by little dots that look like pollen or motes of dust or tiny insects flying over the lawn; he loves the polar light of winter that illuminates effortlessly from behind an overcast sky while under the sheets of that same winter there's a candle that glimmers on the inflamed lips of sex. Perhaps, in reality, everything can be summed up with a principle it is necessary to assume in all its radical simplicity: how could one not love light.

Only the cat notices the presence of the observer, who remains in the doorway. The man showers slowly. He puts anti-inflammatory cream on his arm—the black color has given way to an aubergine purple with small yellow islets. He draws back the curtains. He spends the rest of the afternoon cleaning the house. He tells himself the next occupant should find a place that is tidy, or at least devoid of the remains of his clumsiness and neglect. He applies himself to this task with rare determination.

He opens the windows, cleans the furniture, shakes out the carpets, disinfects the bathroom. The worst part is the kitchen. He fills three garbage bags with cans of expired food and grease-stained rags. The cat watches his efforts with surprise, especially when he moves the wardrobe to clean the balls of fluff. The cat doesn't fail to notice the sluggish walk of the succubus, which, ousted from its hiding place, moves toward the porch. It tries to hide and follow the line of the floor, clinging to the wall. The afternoon light illuminates it with the consistency of cartilage. It reaches the fence with the tired flapping of a chicken that has fallen out of its nest. It tries to propel itself up to the lowest branches of the trees, unsuccessfully. Lying in wait, the cat dilates its pupils. It doesn't hesitate when the time to jump comes, and the succubus knows it is dead before the animal traps it in its claws. Encouraged by this successful outcome, the cat feels an irrepressible desire to mark a territory that has recently been tarnished by too many visitors. Its old, neutered-cat's pride causes it to arch its tail and expel a jet of urine onto the garden fence in the knowledge that the odorous molecules of its urine will be transported far away, further even than the ravine and the gas station, by that pleasant wind coming from the north and refreshing its hindquarters.

The mess in the garden is still visible. He wonders whether he should recover the hydrangeas. He doubts the new owner will waste his time experimenting with grafting plants. He may not even like the country, and live with his back to the forest. He imagines a man aged about forty-five who has made his fortune on the stock market and buys without asking too many questions, having weighed above any other consideration the likely return on his property investment. Perhaps his family will occupy the house for a time, and in the living room there will be conversations, children's cries, a rubber ball bouncing on the floor upstairs. This option strikes him as less gloomy than the image of bare walls and the dirty silhouettes of picture frames that have been removed, a desolate room that would appeal to nothing and nobody. A place that nobody sees, that therefore does not exist, and that nobody redeems with their gaze. A forgotten place.

He sweeps the leaves covering the porch and piles them up in the middle of the garden. He gathers the pages of Laura's diary and lets them fall, one by one, onto the stubble. He examines his heart and the pile of leaves at one and the same time. There is no gesture that indicates mourning, only relief and affirmation. He wonders when he last made a bonfire. He doesn't remember. He brings the flame of the lighter closer, and the fire quickly ignites. A gray smoke smelling of tinder rises through the vents of the leaves. The combustion emerges in lively flames, accompanied by merry crackling, and a slightly bitter air lifts up small sparks and very thin fragments of charred paper. The bonfire spreads an ancient fragrance over the garden. He sits down on the deckchair. He still has a few things to do—take down the for-sale sign, for example, clean the fridge, take out the garbage bags, buy a loaf of bread, perhaps—but he decides to wait for the bonfire to go out completely.

You would have to be an anonymous observer to keep in time with the undulation of the air, that kind of breath now invading everything, and to noiselessly take off from the house, though the cat, leaping onto the man's lap, senses him in the background, with the exact urgency required by a presence it is necessary to identify among the shadows—an anonymous observer that has merged with the smoke now climbing up through the lowest branches of the oaks, rising, and then dissolving at a sufficient height to perhaps see, down below, a man stroking a cat on a deckchair, and a house that is a dot of light, a tiny relief in the now almost nocturnal topography of the valley.

ABOUT THE AUTHOR

JUAN GRACIA ARMENDÁRIZ (Pamplona, 1965) is a Spanish fiction writer and contributor to many Spanish newspapers. He has also been part-time professor at the Universidad Complutense of Madrid, and has many works of literary and documentary research.

As a writer, he has published a book of poems, short stories, non-fiction books—biographical sketches and a historical story—and several novels. *The Plimsoll Line* is part of the "Trilogy of Illness", formed by three separate books that reflect his experience as a person with kidney trouble. The novel was awarded the X Premio Tiflos de Novela 2008.

ABOUT THE TRANSLATOR

JONATHAN DUNNE translates from the Bulgarian, Catalan, Galician and Spanish languages. He has translated work by Tsvetanka Elenkova, Alicia Giménez-Bartlett, Lois Pereiro, Carme Riera, Manuel Rivas and Enrique Vila-Matas among others. He has edited and translated a two-volume *Anthology of Galician Literature* 1196-1981 / 1981-2011 for the Galician publishers Edicións Xerais and Editorial Galaxia and a supplement of *Contemporary Galician Poets* for the UK magazine *Poetry Review*. He has written two books about language and translation—*The DNA of the English Language* and *The Life of a Translator*—as well as the poetry collection *Even Though That*. He directs the publishing house Small Stations Press.

Lightning Source UK Ltd.
Milton Keynes UK
UKOW04f0606040315

247234UK00002B/2/P